MW00415490

THIRD TIME'S A CHARM

A PARANORMAL WOMEN'S FICTION ROMANCE NOVEL

MICHELLE M. PILLOW

MICHELLEPILLOW.COM

Third Time's A Charm © Copyright 2020 by Michelle M. Pillow

First Printing March 26, 2020

Published by The Raven Books LLC

ISBN 9781625012456

ABOUT THE BOOK

Friends don't let friends séance drunk.

Vivien Stone lost the love of her life over twenty years ago. Now that she's in her forties with a string of meaningless relationships under her belt, she can't help but pine for what might have been. It doesn't help that she's somewhat psychic and can pretty much predict where a relationship is heading before it even starts.

When she and her best friends find a hidden book of séances, Vivien believes it's the perfect opportunity to talk to her lost love. But things don't go as planned and what was meant to be a romantic reunion takes a turn for the bizarre.

Maybe some things (and people) are better left buried in the past, and what she really needs has been standing in front of her all along.

AUTHOR UPDATES

Join the Reader Club Mailing List to stay informed
about new books, sales, contests and preorders!

http://michellepillow.com/author-updates/

First, thank you to everyone who helped to get this book out by its scheduled release date during a challenging time in the current global landscape. I'll be the first to admit, this story almost did not make its release date. I know it has been difficult to concentrate on work with so many worries. You all rock!

To my readers and their families, my heart is with all of you. I hope you are all staying safe and healthy during this global pandemic. I know it's been hard, and I thank you for your support of my books and me during this time. Your friendships do not go unnoticed.

AUTHOR NOTE

Being an author in my 40s, I am thrilled to be a part of this Paranormal Women's Fiction #PWF project. Older women kick ass. We know things. We've been there. We are worthy of our own literature category. We also have our own set of issues that we face— empty nests, widows, divorces, menopause, health concerns, etc—and these issues deserve to be addressed and embraced in fiction.

Growing older is a real part of life. Women friendships matter. Women matter. Our thoughts and feelings matter.

If you love this project as much as I do, be sure to spread the word to all your reader friends and let the vendors where you buy your books know you want to see a special category listing on their sites for 40+ heroines in Paranormal Women's Fiction and Romance.

Happy Reading!
Michelle M. Pillow

"Michelle M. Pillow's Second Chance Magic is full of delicious secrets! What's not a secret is how much you're going to love this book and this heroine. I'll take book two now!" - *Kristen Painter, USA TODAY Bestselling Author*

"Delightfully heartfelt and filled with emotion. Psychic powers, newly discovered magic, and a troublesome ex who comes back from the grave. Michelle M. Pillow delivers a wonderfully humorous start to a new paranormal women's fiction romance series." - *Robyn Peterman, NY Times and USA TODAY Bestselling Author*

CHAPTER ONE
FREEWILD COVE HOSPITAL

SAM WAS the only man she would ever love. Vivien had married him the second she'd turned eighteen. He had been nineteen. They were high school sweethearts and everyone told them they were too young to make such a decision. Yes, they were young, but Vivien had never been surer of anything in her life.

The moment she'd met Sam, the very moment, a bolt of lightning had zapped through her. Every psychic sense in her body had lit with fire and every vision she had was vibrant. He was her true love. This was the one man in the world who could love and understand her, and accept everything about her without hesitance or doubt, and worship her as she worshiped him.

Fate.

Destiny.

A sign from the gods.

Whatever you wanted to call it, that was what Vivien had with Sam. He was the other piece of her soul. There would be no one else because there couldn't be.

Vivien had spent her childhood hearing stories of the legendary romances of her gifted ancestors, the kind of tales that defied all logic and social expectations. They all ended in one of two ways—happiness or despair. Which you received was as random as the flip of a coin.

The first way, happiness, was exemplified by her great-grandmother, who had worked at a carnival as a fortune teller. Her specialty had been tarot cards, and one evening she had been asked to read the fortune of an engaged man. The moment she laid eyes on him, she knew he was her true love. She saw the misery in his cards if he continued down the wrong path and warned him. Of course, he'd been angry, but he came back a week later with flowers to apologize. He'd broken things off with his fiancée, after which the woman had confessed to cheating on him. Her great-grandparents had loved each other steadily their entire lives and died in each other's arms.

Her great-great-grandmother had not been so lucky. She, too, had known the love of her life the second she met him. Their hands had touched by accident, and that was it. The world had shifted for both of them, and they had never been the same. They had married, and two years later, her great-great-grandfather had been shot in the heart. Her great-great-grandmother had spent the rest of her life alone, covered in a veil of sadness.

Vivien and Sam had such grand plans. Sam would play his guitar, trying to get gigs at some of the local beach bars. She'd sing, or waitress, or simply stand in the front row dancing. They'd travel the coast in a van, sleeping in the back until they made it big. He was her entire world. He was her heart.

But she was not one of the lucky ones. Her heart was dying, and all she could do was watch.

That was the downside of having a soul mate. Sometimes, life took them away too soon, and then there would be only despair, for how could you find happiness if your heart had died? The psychic abilities that ran through the females in her family also cursed them because it took away all doubts, and in doing so, for some, it took away all hope. If the love of her life died, she would never love again, not like this, not so deep or so sure. Nothing would ever compare.

3

If ever there were proof that the gods were cruel, this was it. After only four years of marriage—the last one of which had been spent in and out of this hospital—Sam was dying from leukemia. She'd begged the universe for mercy when he was going through the various treatments. The universe did not respond.

Vivien had watched as he became too weak to hold his guitar. She'd felt the frailty in his cracked lips when kissing her became too painful to endure. Even holding her hand had been unbearable for him, until the morphine kicked in. Now he wasn't even aware she sat next to him, as his mind drifted in a sea of confusion, and he mumbled incoherent things. She had the impression he was desperate to tell her something, but the thoughts never made it past the painkiller haze.

All she could do was wait.

Each second dug at her heart.

The beep of the machine next to the bed kept a steady rhythm. It had become the soundtrack to the last moments. Vivien knew it would be soon. The clarity of that thought made her hate her psychic gifts.

They had said, "I love you," a million times. She didn't need him to repeat it to know. The beeps felt as if they became louder, causing her to jerk slightly with each one.

"Don't go, baby. Find a way to stay with me," she begged in a hushed whisper.

When she looked at him, she could still see the man she loved hidden in the withered mass of his body. He'd always been so healthy and strong, but cancer had won, and now he was nothing but skin and bones.

"This isn't the end of our story. It can't be," she insisted.

Sam's eyes opened as if he'd heard her. The drugs had given his dark pupils a glassy appearance. His lips moved, but no sound came out.

Vivien leaned over him, turning her ear toward his mouth to better hear what he tried to say. Her brunette hair fell next to him. She brushed the length over her shoulder to keep it from his face. "What is it? What can I get you?"

"There is only us," he whispered.

Her breath caught, but she managed to answer, "Only our hearts."

"I'll be watching you. Save your heart for me. It's mine." The last word was clipped short as a strange gurgle erupted from his lips. She cried out softly as

5

she turned to look at his face. His eyes stared into nothingness.

The monitor beeped a loud, solid tone. She felt people rushing in around her. Someone pulled her arm to move her out of the way so they could work. Vivien stood near the bed, staring for the peaks of her husband she could see through the commotion.

She knew the nurses moved partly out of habit, partly out of pity. There was nothing anyone could do to stop death. Even if they could revive him, Sam wouldn't want that.

Vivien wanted to scream but instead bottled the sound inside her chest. The pain was unbearable, and she was confident she'd follow him into the afterlife.

"I'll be watching you. Save your heart for me. It's mine."

His last words played in her head.

"I'll be watching you."

"It's mine."

"Viv?" Heather Warrick, her best friend, appeared in the doorway. Tears filled her eyes as she looked from Vivien to Sam. She was one of the only people who could have grounded Vivien in that moment. "Oh, no. No."

Heather shook her head as if she could erase what was happening.

The nurses turned off the monitor alarm, and their movements became less pronounced. Vivien had no words. She might never speak again. Any second, the ground would open up and swallow her whole. She didn't want to be in this moment.

Heather rushed to her side and wrapped her arms around her, holding her tight to keep her from falling. "I'm so sorry, Viv. This isn't fair. I don't understand why this is happening. This isn't fair."

Vivien pushed away from Heather, stumbled around a nurse, and collapsed on the bed over Sam's frail form. He was still warm, and if she prayed hard enough, maybe the gods would send him back to her.

They did not, and the pain held her locked in place.

"I'll be watching you. Save your heart for me. It's mine."

CHAPTER TWO
FREEWILD COVE, NORTH CAROLINA

TWENTY YEARS LATER...

Vivien Stone had always believed in magic, in possibilities, in sturdy friendships over popularity. She believed in those things that couldn't be seen, the psychic threads that joined everyone and everything. Secrets pulsed through those threads like blood through veins, completely invisible to most. But if you knew how to listen, if you knew how to look, you could hear those secrets whispering. It was her grandmother who had taught her how to listen before she'd died. All the women in her family had the ability to some extent.

Vivien's daughter would have had the ability... if she'd ever had a daughter.

At forty-two, Vivien knew her childbearing ship

had sailed. Yes, technically, she had all the baby-making equipment, but that was a door she'd never opened. She liked children, and if life had worked out differently, she might have given motherhood a go.

She glanced at her surroundings and shifted uncomfortably in her seat. What was it about this posh waiting room that made her thoughts run in that direction? After Sam died, she'd hit the snooze button on her biological clock and had rarely thought about it again.

Vivien had been in love precisely one time in her life. Sam Stone. He'd been a beautiful man with a heart big enough to love the entire world, and Vivien had been crazy about him. They would stay up all night on the beach with a campfire, Sam playing guitar while she sang. They had made love in the sand—not advisable unless a person enjoyed the feel of sandpaper between the cheeks, but they'd been young and hadn't cared. He was her one true love. It was unfair how fast cancer had taken him from her, but even death and time had not changed her feelings for him.

Incidentally, she'd been in love once, but she'd been married twice. Her second husband, Rex Hewitt, had been a marriage of understanding.

They'd shared a strong affection between them, but not that mad, passionate, soul-altering love. It made sense at the time. Sam had been dead for six years, and Vivien had been twenty-eight and lonely. Rex had felt he needed a pretty wife to advance his career at the law firm of Jerkface, Expensive, and Spray Tan.

Johansen, Elliot, and Snyder lived up to her nicknames for them, and they had been Rex's idols. That probably should have been her first clue the union was doomed from the start. Instead, she'd ignored her psychic alarm bells.

Vivien knew going into the marriage that Rex was incapable of loving anyone more than himself. In her young and stupid decision-making process, that had been what she'd liked about him. There had been no danger of hurting him.

Again, she freely admitted her decision-making process in her twenties left a lot to be desired.

Too bad that hadn't worked both ways. Rex might not have been her true love, but catching her husband cheating on her with three women at the same time still stung.

"Viv, so good to see you." Harry Snyder's voice drew her from her thoughts. She pushed up from the cushioned black seat and met his extended hand with her own. The orange tint to his skin was beyond unnatural, and she wasn't sure why a friend hadn't pulled him aside before now to tell him that carrot wasn't a flattering human shade.

As his hand clasped hers, she had her answer. This man didn't have any real friends. He was incapable.

Her psychic senses picked up on his energy and she instantly wanted hand sanitizer. It wouldn't do anything to get rid of the heebie-jeebies, but it would make her feel better. Ever since she'd found a magical ring left to her by her best friend's grand-mother, Vivien's abilities had been amplified. Things it would normally take concentration to know were flying into her head at a rate she couldn't control.

In no reality did she want to know that Harry liked to be humiliated by prostitutes. Or that he secretly liked the sickly-sweet smell of rotting hamburger meat.

Vivien pulled her hand from his and slowly flexed her fingers. "Rex called and asked me to stop by today. Is he in?"

The elevators dinged, and Harry automatically stopped their fake pleasantries as he turned to greet the arriving gentleman. "Loren, good to see you, sir. I've been meaning to call you to set up a golf game."

Vivien had been divorced for seven years, but every time she came to these offices, she felt as if it had been yesterday. Harry hadn't been so friendly sitting across from her during her divorce. It was only because she'd had pictures of Rex and three highly flexible women that she'd been offered a nice alimony package in exchange for her silence.

The firm frowned upon public moral embarrassments, but instead of firing Rex, they'd closed ranks around him. Vivien knew for a fact they'd had her followed for months. She couldn't prove it and had no evidence that would stand up in court, but she *knew*. Just like she knew the office manager had been keeping tabs on her from the moment she'd walked in, even when she pretended not to be paying attention.

Vivien glanced at the office manager talking on the phone where the receptionist should have been. Mrs. Cameron worked for the firm since the dawn of time. Her matronly attitude and sharp memory had impressed Vivien until she realized one of Mrs. Cameron's main duties was balancing wives and mistresses... and she didn't appear to lose any sleep over it. Like some mob numbers guy with two sets of accounting books, Mrs. Cameron kept two sets of calendars for each lawyer in the firm.

Vivien slowly went back to her chair. Before she was fully reseated, Harry turned to her.

"Ready?" Harry asked.

Vivien pushed up mid-sit and nodded. Her heels were uncomfortable, and she hated that she'd been compelled to wear them, but they matched her trendy business suit. The flowing pants and jacket were more fashionable than practical.

Harry stopped at a conference room and held open the door for her to walk in first.

Vivien glanced at the empty table inside and frowned. "Where's Rex?"

"Why don't we go in and have a seat."

Vivien hated the placating tone of his voice. He was one head pat away from calling her a little lady. She bit her tongue and kept from responding. The jackass couldn't help himself any more than he could end his addiction to huffing spray tanner.

Vivien brushed past him and stood by the walnut conference table. Folders with her name on them had been laid out. A tiny thread of annoyance and dread filled her to see them. "What is this about? Where is Rex? I'm here as a courtesy because he kept leaving me messages begging me to come. I don't appreciate being made to wait for a half hour."

"Please have a seat." Harry gestured to a chair.

Vivien arched a brow and stared at him for a few seconds before placing her purse on the conference table and finally taking a seat. He sat opposite her and slid the folders in front of him. Placing his hand on the stack, he said, "Thank you for coming in, Vivien. We appreciate you making this easier for us."

We? Us? Unless this man had an imaginary friend, they were the only two in the room.

"Why are *we* here?" Vivien asked, leaning onto her arms as she met his gaze. The hard wood was chilled from being under the air conditioning vent.

"It has been seven years since your divorce with my client," Harry said, his tone changing to a more formal cadence.

"I'm aware. I was there."

"You were only married seven years," Harry continued.

"Also aware, also there," Vivien said, her annoyance growing. She had better things to do than have this not-so-lovely stroll down memory lane.

"It is our feeling that Rex has been more than generous in regard to alimony payments. In most cases, alimony for marriages that last under ten years are for only half of the time married, so three and a half years in your case." Rex opened the top file and ran his finger down the page as if to confirm what he

15

wished to discuss. Vivien knew the act was all for show. Harry knew what he wanted to say.

"Your point?" she asked.

"Would you agree it's been more than fair?" Harry prompted.

Rex used to try to manipulate her like that. He'd ask a series of questions to get her to say yes to things so psychologically she'd be primed to say yes to the thing he *really* wanted.

"Why am I here?" Vivien leaned back and crossed her arms over her chest.

Rex looked at his page. "You receive thirty-five percent of his income. I would say that has been more than generous."

"Is he looking for a thank you card?" Vivien quipped. She had no clue what this ambush meeting was about, but she could psychically pick up Harry's lunch order. Why was her gift so useless right now? Regardless, it had quickly become apparent that Rex wasn't going to grow a pair and face her. "Rex offered the thirty-five percent."

"In North Carolina, it's unusual for a—"

"Harry, I'm going to stop you right there. My lawyer told me that in this state and under my particular circumstances I could have easily pushed for forty percent, so one could argue that *I* was very generous. Now, either you get to the point, or I'm leaving. You're acting like Rex needs a liver transplant." Vivien felt the man's mounting frustration, even though he schooled his expression.

Rex had never believed her when she said she had psychic abilities. In fact, the term he used was nutjob. Vivien didn't need her ex-husband to believe her. She knew she was clairsentient. When she was with someone, she could pick up on what they were feeling. She also happened to be claircognizant and often knew things without knowing how she knew them.

Like now.

"It's not a liver transplant, is it? He's in line for a promotion." Vivien gave a small laugh, secretly grateful that her gift had finally given her something useful. "Are you making him a full partner?"

"Let's stay on topic, please. We're going to petition the court to end alimony payments. We feel—"

"We? Don't you mean *Rex* feels?" Vivien inserted.

"We feel that fourteen years of compensation for a seven-year marriage is excessive." Harry tapped his pointer finger on his stack of files.

"Fourteen? Did you seriously just imply that I was compensated *during* my marriage, as well as after?" Vivien shook her head. She kept her tone light, mostly to annoy him, as she added, "That's insulting not only to me but to every married and formerly married woman in the world, and it cheapens wives to no more than prostitutes. Do you think wives are prostitutes, Harry?"

"I misspoke. Of course, I meant seven." Harry was unable to hide his frustrated reaction to that comment. Some things she didn't need to be psychic to see. "This is a courtesy meeting to give you the chance to sign away further payments without having to go to court."

Wow. This guy had a giant set of balls. He talked like he was doing her a favor.

"You have had ample time to find meaningful employment," he continued, "and a new residence if the mortgage payments continue to be a financial burden."

That was something her lawyer had asserted in the divorce proceedings—financial burden.

These people acted like all the things she'd done to help Rex's career were nothing. It wasn't just decorating his house, hosting parties, and being his plus one at endless dinners. She'd drafted half his legal arguments, including the one that set him on the partner track.

Vivien pulled her purse from the table onto her lap. She dug for her phone and clutched it in her hand. "Well, since it has been seven long years like you so eagerly keep pointing out today, let me remind you why Rex offered me alimony in the first place." She glanced down at her phone and tapped the screen to bring up a passworded folder. She clicked on the first picture and held it up so he could see. "I'm no attorney, but I believe the term my lawyer used when he saw these was marital misconduct."

Harry glanced at the picture and his eyes widened.

"You didn't see these during negotiations, did you?" Vivien leaned forward and angled her phone so they could both watch what she was doing. "Here's Rex with three prostitutes. Though, between us, I think they're all faking those expressions." She slid to the next shot. "And Rex trying on that woman's clothes and makeup. Fishnets are not an easy look to pull off." She scrolled to the next one. Vertical blinds blurred part of the picture, but there was enough of the seedy motel room visible to show a camcorder pointed at the bed. "Here's Rex recording himself. You'd think a lawyer would know better."

"I don't see what—"

"Oh, wait, I have the actual video." Vivien moved

to the next file. "After the private detective I hired showed me the photos he took, I recognized what looked like our personal camcorder in some of them. It didn't take long to find the rest of the evidence I needed. But here, watch for yourself. As my lawyer liked to tell me, solid proof plays out so much better in court than hearsay, and people just love watching videos. It's like reality television."

She pushed play. The sounds that came from her phone belonged in a porno. Then again, that was exactly what the video was—amateur porn. Vivien was no prude, but she had never let Rex record them in bed.

"Hold on, let me fast forward to my favorite part." Vivien ran her finger over the screen until she found what she wanted. She zoomed in and held the phone close to his face. "I believe that's cocaine Rex is snorting off that young lady's very trim backside." She moved the screen view. "And that's a coffee mug with the law firm logo." She moved it again to show the full shot. "The private detective told me that one of these girls was only twenty. So I'm guessing when he pours them shots later and serves her liquor, that's a bad thing."

Either Harry had thought she'd lost the evidence,

or he had not realized how bad it made Rex look. "You can't prove when that was taken."

"I suppose the time stamp on the camcorder could have been faked, but at about twenty minutes in you can hear the newscaster talk about a book launch party for a local author, which proves when it was taken." She held her phone in front of her and hovered her finger. "Do you want me to find it for you?"

Harry refused her offer with a firm shake of his head. "No. I don't need to see more."

"Drugs, alcohol, prostitutes, adultery." Vivien turned off the video, unable to continue listening to the sex noises. "It doesn't look very good for your new partner, Harry. But you do what you have to do. We can go to court, show the judge, and let him decide what I deserve for putting *my* career on hold to help Rex with his, for being faithful, and throwing parties to entertain law firm clients. I might just ask for forty percent this time instead of thirty-five. There is a lot of pain and suffering in this video that I will have to live through. Not to mention my humiliation when this goes public."

"Well, like you said, you'd be humiliated." Harry clung to the only threat he had.

Vivien nodded. "You're right. Maybe I should ask for fifty percent."

Harry stared at her phone like he contemplated grabbing it and smashing it.

"Don't worry," Vivien said. "I have backup copies. If Rex wants to stroll down memory lane, I'll be happy to email him the file."

Harry shut the top folder and slid it aside. "I don't see any need for dramatics." He opened the next one. "We were worried you might not see things our way, so we drafted a settlement of a one-time payment that is more than generous. Rex just wants to get on with his life. I'm sure you do too."

Harry turned the folder and slid it toward her. Vivien leaned forward to read, "*One hundred fifty thousand dollars.*"

Vivien laughed. "Why would I do that? Our divorce states that I am to be paid thirty-five percent of Rex's salary."

"Yes, thirty-five of his salary at the time of the divorce," Harry answered.

"That might have been what Rex wanted, but that's not what was written down. You might have to fire an intern because what we signed and filed said I get thirty-five percent, period. So unless that third file on the table is telling me what kind of a raise we're getting with his new promotion, I think I'm done with this conversation." Vivien stood. "Tell your client that the next time he wants me to meet with his lawyer, be upfront about it, and call my attorney first."

"Do you really need all that money?" Harry insisted. "Can't you be reasonable about this, Viv?"

"Call me Mrs. Stone," she corrected. They weren't friends. "Now, if you would excuse me, I am taking care of an injured friend and I need to get home."

Vivien strode to the door and opened it.

Before she left, she glanced back. "Exactly how big is this raise?"

Harry didn't meet her eyes.

"That's all right. I'll just look at the statements that come with the next payment notice. I'm thinking it might be time to have my attorney do an audit of the funds I'm receiving, just to make sure there are no clerical errors. Consider this a courtesy notice to get your paperwork in order. It worries me that you thought it was thirty-five percent of his salary from seven years ago. If there have been any raises, I hope you weren't sending the wrong amount all these years." Vivien kept her head high as she strode away from the conference room.

Rex could kiss her ass. Except for the first couple of years when she'd invested the alimony payments into property and franchises, almost all of what he gave her went to charities each month, and several of them had come to depend on the donations. It was Vivien's way of keeping karma balanced for all the bad shit Rex put out into the world.

She walked by Mrs. Cameron at the reception desk, moving past the woman to go down the hall toward the last place she knew Rex to have an office.

"Wait, you can't go back there," Mrs. Cameron called after her.

Vivien walked faster. She stopped by the door that read, "*Rex Hewitt,*" in bold letters and looked through the blinds at the desk inside the office. Aside from the shift his hair had undergone from black to gray, he looked the same. She always found it to be a shame that a person's face didn't always match their insides. Rex had the kind of silver fox features that only looked better with age.

Vivien rapped on the window with her knuckle. The ring on her forefinger struck the glass.

His hands were wrapped around a giant sandwich, and he was mouth deep in a bite when his brown eyes met hers. He visibly stiffened.

Vivien arched a brow and flipped him off, mouthing, "Coward."

"You can't be—" Mrs. Cameron rushed toward her.

"Take it easy, Gal Friday," Vivien quipped, cutting off the woman's words. "I was just leaving."

Vivien heard the ding of an elevator and hurried to catch it before it closed. The less time she spent on this floor, the better. When Rex had called, begging her to come by and talk, she hadn't thought he'd meant to drag her into a legal mess. She should have realized it, but she hadn't. Her psychic gift didn't work over the telephone.

She didn't look to see if the elevator was going up or down. All she saw was the doors closing, and she rushed forward to slip her hand into the opening to trip the sensors.

The doors opened. A man in a business suit looked annoyed by the delay. His hair had enough gel in it that the lines from his comb were still noticeable.

The woman next to Mr. Hair Gel gave her a faint smile. She leaned against the handrail with her arms crossed over her chest.

Vivien hesitated. A small shiver worked over her as she met the woman's green eyes, and she felt a little sick to her stomach.

"Well?" the man asked.

Vivien stepped forward slowly, a little light-headed. For such a small space, there was a lot of psychic energy floating around the elevator.

"Vivien?" She had not seen the third passenger on the elevator right away.

"Oh, hey," she answered. Her new neighbor, Troy Radford, was a professor on sabbatical to write a book on an anthropological study of modern beach culture and its impact on the environment... or something academically worthwhile like that. Every time he tried to talk to her, she'd found an excuse to leave the area.

It wasn't that the guy creeped her out. In fact, it was quite the opposite. Troy had an approachable smile with traces of laugh lines that proved he used it often. His shorter dark hair had hints of steely gray, and his dark eyes would be easy to get lost in.

In her mind, male college professors always wore slacks and sweater vests. She had no clue why, but it was the image she associated with them—admittedly unfairly. Troy did not fit that mold. His lightweight linen shirts were button-down, but not sharply pressed. More often than not, he was in cargo pants or jeans with sneakers.

"How've you been?" she asked Troy, not looking at him.

Vivien glanced at the woman's reflection in the metal elevator door. She didn't like the vibe she picked up. It wasn't the woman, per se, but something that floated around her.

"Good, thanks," Troy answered. "I finally got most of my boxes unpacked. You know what they say. If they're not unpacked after a month, you probably don't need it."

"Is that what they say?" Vivien didn't pay attention to the conversation. Troy was a nice enough man, but the second he'd introduced himself, she knew that he wanted to ask her out on a date. She found it best to avoid him.

Having psychic tendencies could be fun, but for the most part it was a great survival tool. Troy was the type to want a relationship, something deep and meaningful. He was the kind to have an eye on marriage. Vivien had been there, done that two times. She wasn't interested in going for round three. That was why she preferred dating the younger men who came to Freewild Cove on vacation. They came pre-installed with commitment phobias and a timetable.

Plus, some of them, for the briefest of flashes, reminded her of Sam. She lived for those fleeting moments. She would give anything to see Sam again, hold him, hear him, kiss him. Time had faded some of the details, but that feeling of acceptance and all-consuming love lingered. The ache was deep and had been with her so long that she wasn't sure what life would be like without it.

The elevator dinged, and the woman and Mr. Hair Gel made a move to exit at the same time. Vivien grabbed the woman by her upper arm to stop her. At the contact, the woman looked more surprised than concerned.

"That man is going to try to share a cab with you. Say no. Trust me. You're not safe with him." Vivien released the woman's arm and couldn't blame her when she rushed away from the crazy lady telling her what to do.

"Do you know that guy?" Troy asked.

Vivien shook her head in denial. "No. Never seen him before."

"Then...?" Troy watched as the woman left the building. Mr. Hair Gel had stopped a cab and stood with the door open. He gestured toward the lady as if offering to share a ride. His wide smile made Vivien press her lips together as she watched with bated breath.

The woman glanced back toward the building,

appearing worried. She slowly shook her head and headed off in the opposite direction on foot.

Vivien released her breath and whispered to herself, "Good girl."

"Wait, how did you...?" Troy moved to hold open the front door for her. "Why didn't you want her to share a cab with that man?"

"I don't know. Just a feeling." Vivien didn't want to get into details about what it meant to be claircognizant. She'd tried to tell people she was psychic in the past, especially when she was younger, and people had one of two reactions. Rarely, they believed her and then wanted her to predict stuff for them. Or, usually, they didn't believe her and they treated her like a kooky freak. Since some of her ancestors used to work as tarot card readers on the carnival circuit in the late 1800s and early 1900s, the word *freak* had been a family curse word on par with dropping an f-bomb.

The truth was, Vivien didn't know *how* she knew. She saw the two of them, knew he'd try to give the woman a ride, and knew it would be unfortunate if the woman went with him. She had no clue why it would be bad or what exactly would happen.

"Are you heading home?" Troy asked.

"Um, yeah." Vivien nodded as she reached into her purse to find her keys.

"I don't suppose you'd want to share a cab with me? I promise I won't give off any feelings." Troy was clearly trying to make a joke.

With the woman gone, the feeling of dread began to evaporate, and she was able to give Troy more of her attention. She smiled. "Thanks, but I have a car."

Vivien started to turn, only to remember her manners.

"Would you like a ride home?" she asked. It occurred to her that it would look rude if she pulled into her driveway at the same time his cab arrived. "I need to pick up dinner first. I have a friend staying with me. Lorna hasn't been feeling very well. Another friend is joining us."

Why was she supplying all this extra information?

"Oh? Nothing serious I hope." Troy fell into step next to her, clearly taking her up on her offer for a ride.

"Lorna..." Vivien tried to think of an eloquent way of explaining that she'd gotten drunk with two of her friends and they'd accidentally séanced a demon using an old book of magic they'd found hidden beneath the stage of the historic movie theater. Her best friend, Heather Harrison, owned the theater, which she'd inherited from her grandmother, Julia Warrick.

Julia had been a renowned medium. People had traveled miles to go to her shows and paid her to talk to their loved ones. They were learning how to do seances from Julia's magic book. Ghost Julia had also gifted Vivien, Lorna, and Heather with the magical rings they now wore.

"Lorna?" Troy prompted when she didn't finish her sentence.

"Oh, sorry," Vivien mumbled, realizing in her attempt to come up with an answer, she'd forgotten to actually give one. "Lorna was attacked. She'll be fine."

"Seriously?" Troy frowned. "Did it happen here in town? Is she all right? I don't remember reading about an attack. Did they catch who did it?"

That was a lot of questions.

"I don't want to talk about it," Vivien said. "It's Lorna's business, and I don't feel comfortable talking behind her back."

"Oh, yeah, of course," he said, nodding as if he understood her lame excuse.

Troy felt like someone she wanted to know, and it would be easy—*oh so easy*—to fall into his arms.

The man was attractive, and she was a woman who knew how to make the most out of her attraction. But she also didn't want it to get that far. She wasn't sure why she felt so strongly about that point, but she did. Unless he bluntly asked her out, there would be no reason to turn him down.

She didn't want to date him and break his heart.

She didn't want him to ask her out and for things to become awkward between them.

Friends. Friendship would be good. If she could keep him off the dating track long enough, he'd easily fall into the friend zone. She should say something friendly to him.

"So, which floor were you here for?" She tried to steer the conversation away from her supernatural hobbies.

"Twelfth, rental insurance," Troy answered. "My landlord is insisting I take out a policy."

"Yeah, he gets a referral discount on his own policies if he gets his tenants to do that," Vivien answered.

"You were on eleven, that's the..." He glanced at the building. "Law offices, right?"

"I had to stop in and pay my ex-husband tax," she said.

"Oh, I'm sorry, I didn't realize you were going

through a divorce." Troy watched his feet as he stepped around a cracked section of the concrete parking lot.

"Seven years ago. My ex is a lawyer and has an office here. They wanted me to look at some papers." None of these were things Vivien felt like talking about. She picked up her pace, walking along the parked cars as she looked for the back end of her white sedan. "How's your work coming along?"

"My moving here is really just an excuse to hang at the beach and people watch." Troy laughed.

Vivien found her car and made a beeline for it, hitting the button on her key chain multiple times to unlock the doors before they reached them. The car responded with a loud *ka-thunk, ka-thunk, ka-thunk*.

Normally, her ex didn't get to her. She barely thought about Rex anymore. He was like a bill that needed to be auto drafted to and from her bank account. She knew the monthly annoyance was there, but she didn't think about it unless she was looking directly at it.

"You should join me sometime." Troy had opened the passenger door and leaned against the frame as he looked over the roof of the car. He gave her an easy smile. The man was handsome and definitely attractive, but that didn't change the vibe she got off of him. He was the kind of person who looked for a serious relationship. Vivien wasn't sure she had any room left for one of those.

"Yeah, maybe." It was the politest *no* she could manage at the moment.

As she slid into the driver's seat, she wished he wouldn't have hinted at a date. It only made the car ride potentially awkward. She forced herself to pay closer attention to the conversation so she could steer it in the right direction—away from hints of dating.

Friend zone. Find the friend zone.

"That's an interesting ring." Troy nodded toward her hand.

Vivien automatically looked down, even though she knew what the antique jewelry looked like. "Thanks. It's one of three friendship rings."

But it was more than that. The same night Vivien had found the jewelry hidden away in a storage box, Lorna and Heather had also discovered their rings. Heather had been home alone going through tax receipts, and Lorna had been in her apartment having a self-pity party (her words, not Vivien's) and looking for her old wedding ring.

The second they'd put them on, magical things had started to happen. Vivien's empathic abilities had amped up. Lorna developed the ability to heal herself and others—well, not heal so much as the ability to transfer illnesses and injuries from one person to another. Heather had always been able to see and hear ghosts, including Grandma Julia, and that hadn't changed.

"Oh, like those novelty rings that fit together like a puzzle? I would have guessed it was antique," he said.

She watched the rearview mirror as cars passed behind her, waiting for her turn to pull out.

"It is. From the early 1900s, I think. Julia Warrick, who commissioned the historic theater downtown, was the grandmother of my friend Heather. The rings belonged to her." Vivien glanced at the jewelry, even now feeling a tingle of energy pulsing from it. "Do you have an interest in jewelry?"

"Not particularly." He gave a small smile and laughed as he fastened his seat belt.

"Then what's with all the ring questions?" Vivien took the first break she found in the parking lot traffic to muscle her way between a minivan and a sports car. One look at the latter and she knew the man who owned it was overcompensating for a lack of personality. It wasn't a judgment about the car, which was *sweet as* (like the tour guide from her recent New Zealand trip would have said), but more an observation that proved her psychic abilities were in useless-information overdrive.

"I have an interest in you." Troy again turned his attention to her.

So much for her psychic abilities. While they'd been focused on the douchebag in a sports car, she'd missed Troy's oncoming flirting.

She glanced in his direction, pretending to concentrate on traffic as she eased the car forward. Damn it. Troy had the kind of smiling eyes that set her to tingling. They made her want to gaze back at him. She'd have to be careful around those eyes, and not forget herself.

Dating the serious neighbor would be bad.

Dating studly bar hook-ups... well, also bad, but in an entirely naughty-fun, noncommittal way.

She needed to change the subject. Fast. For some reason she was off her game today. She blamed the surprise attack. She was over Rex, but hearing the sounds of his amateur porn had left a sick feeling in her stomach. It dredged up all the shit she didn't want in her life.

"I hope you like tacos." Vivien furrowed her brows. Yep. That's the conversation change she came up with. Tacos. If she weren't careful, he'd think she was asking *him* on a date. "Since you're new here, I doubt you've found our secret gem, Toco." She glanced at the clock. "We call it that because the A on the sign is faded. This time of day Maria will be parked near the beach."

"Parked? As in a food truck?"

"Not just a food truck. *The* best food truck in the country," Vivien corrected. "Trust me. It's an orgasmic experience."

Well, crap. Mentioning orgasms probably wasn't the best way to get his mind off dating her.

Way to go, Viv.

Dumbass.

Vivien pulled out of the parking lot and stepped on the gas, driving a little too fast as she made her way toward the beach.

CHAPTER THREE

VIVIEN TRIED NOT to sigh in relief as she pulled her car into the driveway. "Well, we're here."

The obvious statement was just one more thing in a string of stupid things she'd said to Troy on the ride home. Her original plan hadn't been to put him off by being a complete dingbat, but to let him down easily in a tactful, intelligent way.

Unfortunately, the dingbat method was how everything seemed to be working out.

What was it about this man that threw her off her game? She wasn't shy when it came to talking to people. Heck, half the time, Heather told her she started a conversation in the middle with strangers and just expected them to go along for the ride. With Troy, nothing came out as planned.

Gah, it was like she was a freshman in high school all over again, saying all the wrong things. Sam had told her it was endearing. Few people had thought so.

Troy had mentioned an author, and she'd said she didn't read. It was a blatant lie when there was no reason to lie about it. Authors were a safe conversation to have.

He mentioned baseball, and she said she didn't care for sports. Not exactly a lie. She didn't like a lot of sports, but there was something to be said for a good, sexy Scottish caber toss. Thankfully she didn't start rambling about guys in kilts.

Then, when they finally made it to the taco truck, she'd ordered enough food to feed fifteen friends. Apparently, her subconscious wanted him to think she was having a party and he wasn't invited. That, or she was going to spend the night binge-eating thirty tacos plus extras.

"Thanks for the ride." Troy reached for the handle. He carried a small takeout bag as he climbed out of the car. He didn't meet her gaze.

Vivien frowned at his back. As his door shut, she quickly got out of the car and said, "I lied before. I read. Books. Sometimes. I like thrillers."

He turned, appearing confused. "Okay?"

40

"Earlier, when we were driving, you were talking about a class you had to teach and asked if I had read Proust, and I told you I didn't read. I meant I didn't read Proust, or I don't read him—I mean, I have. I found him dull. I like thrillers."

"No Proust. Got it." He gave her a tight smile, the kind you give someone to humor them. He lifted his to-go bag in a small wave. "Thanks again for the ride and showing me where to track down the best tacos in the universe."

Yep, he was humoring her. He hadn't even tried one of the tacos yet.

Vivien opened her mouth, trying to think of something to redeem herself. Nothing came out.

"Is there anything else?" he asked.

"I..." She glanced at the house. "My friends are expecting me."

Vivien opened the back car door and pulled out the giant bag of food. She didn't look back as she rushed toward her front steps.

Well, she had wanted to put him off the idea of asking her out on a date. Mission accomplished. At this rate, she'd be lucky if he'd want to hold a conversation with her again. Dust bunnies were more articulate than she had been.

"I thought you were going to see your ex." Lorna

Addams stood at Vivien's living room window over-looking the driveway. Hints of bruises still discolored the woman's arms. Her long brown hair had streaks of reddish-blonde highlights and was pulled up into a messy bun on the top of her head. A few locks fell around her shoulders.

Lorna favored wearing jeans and t-shirts to dressing up. It was that easygoingness that had first caught Vivien's attention. Lorna wasn't the type of woman who fussed with herself. Her attention was focused on what she was doing, on taking care of others, on the job at hand. It was no wonder Lorna's new psychic powers came in the form of finding and healing.

"I was." Vivien adjusted the heavy bag of food from her hip to balance the weight on her arms in front of her. She might have over-ordered, but when it came to entertaining, she would rather have too much food than not enough. "Or I thought I was. Rex had me ambushed by his lawyer."

"Really?" Lorna dropped the curtain to look at her. "Why? I thought the divorce was long over."

"It is. Rex is trying to get out of his alimony payments because he's about to make partner, which comes with a raise." Vivien pushed the front door closed with her foot and carried the bag toward the coffee table. She set it down before going to grab plates and napkins from the kitchen.

They'd only been roommates for about two weeks. Before then, Vivien had lived alone. Lorna had been staying in the studio apartment above the Warrick Theater, where she worked as the manager. The apartment came with the job, which would have been great except that the theater had been haunted by the demon they'd summoned while trying to talk to dead loved ones.

Oops.

Vivien was *reasonably* sure they'd sent the demon back to hell, but regardless, Lorna had moved out of the apartment.

Vivien found she enjoyed having company. The house was more space than she needed and had felt empty since she'd won the home in the divorce. She hated how they'd said it like that. *Won* the house, like it was some kind of carnival prize.

The house had not been changed in the seven years since her divorce. She'd left the décor exactly the same—art prints and boring vases, a couch that didn't invite people to sit on it. Everything perfectly matched, measured, and placed. And it was boring as hell. Rex hadn't wanted a home. He wanted a house that could be photographed at a moment's notice. He wanted an event venue near the beach to entertain business associates.

Vivien told herself she'd left it that way as a reminder not to make the same mistake again. In truth, she worried she'd done it as a form of self-punishment for having married a man she didn't love.

"So, if you were with Rex, where did you pick up the hottie?" Lorna asked, pulling back the curtain to check the driveway when Vivien returned from the kitchen. "Do you want me to hide in the guest room so you can be alone with him? I can pretend I'm not here."

"Oh, crap, he's not coming over here, is he?" She dropped the plates and napkins by the food bag.

"Maybe... Wait, no. He just picked up a plastic bottle out of the lawn. It looks like he's going next door," Lorna answered.

"Good," Vivien said. "That's our neighbor, Troy."

"Our neighbor is cute," Lorna said. "You never told me our neighbor was cute."

"Because I thought you were all about dating William," Vivien countered. "You know, William, Heather's brother, the dreamboat who keeps sneaking over every night like I won't notice when he triggers the motion sensors."

Vivien gave a small laugh. She'd known William and Heather since middle school. Lorna was a new friend, but it felt like she'd known her just as long. She was glad William and Lorna were working out as a couple. Lorna had been hurt badly in the past, and William had never known the joy of having his entire world turned upside-down by a woman.

Vivien thought her triple-cheating ex won the asshole prize, but Lorna's dead husband had taken it to the next level. Lorna had found out at the funeral that her husband of twenty years had been hiding another wife. With Lorna, he'd had three kids, a paycheck-to-paycheck lifestyle, and a modest home. With Cheryl, he'd been rich. The bigamy was terrible enough, but it turned out Lorna was the second wife, not the first, and she'd not been entitled to anything but public humiliation.

No, that's not true. Lorna had come out ahead. She was infinitely the better person, and she had her three kids. Fortunately by the time Glenn's secret came out, they were all adults living on their own.

"Does it bother you?" Lorna released the curtain and turned to study her. Vivien was glad that Lorna couldn't read her thoughts.

"That William sets off the motion sensors?" Vivien shrugged. "Not really. I only have them

45

because we occasionally get drunk tourists trying to come through the back gate. I wake up just long enough to check it and ignore it."

"I meant that William is over here all the time?" Lorna asked.

Vivien couldn't stop the laugh that escaped her. She knew Lorna had concerns about Vivien and William's closeness. Yes, the two of them were close —like annoying-brother and awesome-perfect-sister close. But there had been nothing romantic between them.

"I promise you, it doesn't bother me," Vivien said, mostly because she felt like Lorna needed to hear it. "I'm happy for both of you. I like the look I see on your face when he's around. That kind of feeling is worth holding on to with both hands."

"Just *my* face?" Lorna asked. Her husband had done a number on her. Vivien couldn't blame the woman for her trust issues.

"His affection for you is so obvious that it's actually a little embarrassing," Vivien assured her.

Lorna visibly relaxed, and the corner of her lips curled up in a tiny smile.

"What are you doing out of bed? Shouldn't you be resting?" Vivien asked.

"I feel better. Moving around seems to help. Plus,

a woman can only watch so much television and read so many books." She made a point of leaning to the side and bending her knees. "My hip is still a little sore from where I landed on it, but I can tell it's getting better."

It was good to see her friend on her feet. The demon had come after Lorna in two brutal attacks. The first had put her in the hospital. With the second, Lorna had refused to see a doctor for fear of more bills that she couldn't afford.

Before Lorna had been discharged from Freewild Cove Hospital, Vivien had written a check for the bulk of the outstanding balance and ordered Nancy in accounts receivable to hide the payment when it came time to send the billing statement. Lorna had a lot of pride, and she didn't need to know what Vivien had done for her.

Lorna could have healed herself by dispersing her pain over several people, but she refused to harm anyone else, and so she lived with her injuries. With her empathic gift, Vivien could sense how much pain her friend was in. She had tried to convince Lorna to transfer some of the pain to her, but Lorna had declined the offer.

"You never answered about the cute neighbor." Lorna lowered herself onto one of the cream-colored couches and angled her body to take the pressure off her hip. "How is it you're driving around with him?"

"I ran into him outside Rex's office and saved him the cab fare home." Vivien dismissed the teasing tone. "I hope you're hungry. I bought tamales, tacos, taquitos, burritos, churros, street corn, all the food groups."

"Yes, that sounds—" Lorna lifted her hand, touching the large, black stone ring on her forefinger as if sensing the same thing Vivien did. "Heather's here."

A few seconds later, the sound of Heather's car pulled into the drive. Headlights flashed along the windowsill beneath the edge of the curtains even though it was still fairly light outside.

Heather knocked even as she opened the door. Her gaze went to Lorna. "Am I late?"

"Just on time. I went to Toco," Vivien said.

"How are you feeling?" Heather quietly shut the door, not taking her eyes off Lorna. She carried her purse and a messenger bag that appeared weighed down with supplies.

"Much better, thank you," Lorna said.

Heather's dark brown hair hung damp along her back, the weight of the locks only starting to curl. Her flannel shirt looked like what she wore almost every day to work and had probably come from the top of a clean, unfolded laundry basket.

Heather worked harder than anyone Vivien had ever met. She owned properties all over town and was always acquiring more. It hadn't always been like that, but Heather had suffered the kind of loss no person ever should. Working gave Heather a sense of purpose to her day.

"Why are you looking at me like that?" Heather gave Vivien a quizzical smile and brushed her hair behind her ear.

"All work and no play makes Heather a dull girl," Vivien answered.

"Gee, thanks?" Heather laughed. She dropped her purse in a corner on the floor and then sat next to Lorna on the couch. She placed the messenger bag between them. "You appear to be in a mood. I take it the meeting with Rex didn't go well."

"Nothing surprising. He wants out of our alimony deal, but instead of asking like an adult, he tried to have his lawyer intimidate me." Vivien shrugged. "I played the porn tape and threatened to have him audited. So you know, all in all, a very grown-up-mature day."

"She gave the neighbor hottie a ride home," Lorna inserted. "But she doesn't want to talk about that. She keeps changing the subject every time I ask her about it."

"You should let me set you up with Troy," Vivien said. That would solve two problems. Heather might actually do something besides work, and Troy could turn his attentions to someone who could return his feelings. The part of her that was attracted to the hottie neighbor felt a pang of jealousy at the idea, but she would never begrudge Heather her happiness.

"Troy?" Heather looked at Lorna.

"Neighbor hottie," Lorna clarified. She turned her attention to Heather as if the two of them were having a private conversation. "I'm not surprised she's trying to set you up with him. She's trying to pretend she's indifferent, but I think otherwise. Her face was flushed when she came home, and you should have seen the way they were looking at each other when she dropped him off. If I didn't know better, I would say Vivien has a crush."

"Yes, I think you might be right. I sense something is different about her." Heather lifted her fist to show the ring on her forefinger as she pointed it toward Vivien like a magic talisman. "Something has her off-kilter, and I don't believe it's Rex being Rex."

Lorna balled her fist and pointed her ring at Vivien. "We command you to speak."

"I kind of hate both of you right now." Vivien's ring finger tingled as if energy vibrated from the jewelry. Thankfully, it wasn't enough to make her follow the playful command. She ignored the sensation as she grabbed a cushioned chair and dragged it across the floor to sit beside the coffee table.

"Well, that didn't work," Heather chuckled as if she hadn't expected it to. "I was sure we were due to develop a new superpower. It's not fair, Viv, that you can tell what's going on with me by just looking at me, but we have to pry answers out of you."

"Yes, what are you hiding?" Heather asked. "Spill."

"Lorna exaggerates. If Troy was looking at me in any special way, it was in disgust. I pretended I was a dingbat so he wouldn't ask me out. Are you happy? Now you know everything."

"So you—wait, what?" Heather frowned. "You pretended you were less intelligent to get a man not to ask you out?"

"When you say it like that..." Vivien searched the bag for a beef taco. "Who wants a taco?"

"Since when do you avoid speaking your mind? You are the most forthright person I know. You tell people things when they don't want to hear those things all the time," Heather insisted. "If he asked you out and you're not interested, why wouldn't you just tell him that? Why the game? That's really not like you."

Vivien pulled out a burrito. "Burrito?"

"Viv?" Heather crossed her arms over her chest and arched a brow.

"Fine. I don't know." She waved the wrapped burrito to enunciate her frustration. "It's like I can't get the freaking words out of my freaking throat, and I just say stupid shit. Plus, he's a likable guy, from what little I can pick up from him. I don't want to hurt him."

"And you're attracted to him," Lorna added.

"Fine. Yes." Vivien dropped the burrito on the table and again looked in the bag. "He is an attractive man, but I've told attractive men no before."

"He's not like most of the young men you date," Lorna added.

"Thank you, exactly." Vivien nodded at Lorna.

"I'm not saying that's a good thing," Lorna corrected with a small laugh.

"I am," Vivien quipped, pulling out a taco. She peeled back the wrapper and took a defiant bite.

"I wasn't saying that was a bad thing, either," Lorna corrected. "What I meant was if you like him, maybe it's time to try something different. You deserve to be happy."

"I am happy," Vivien answered. "Men don't define my happiness."

"I didn't mean to imply—" Lorna began.

"She's messing with you," Heather interrupted. "She's not really annoyed. She knows exactly what you meant."

"It's just too easy to tease you sometimes," Vivien laughed.

"Ha, ha," Lorna grumbled, wrinkling her nose in Vivien's direction.

"So he shakes you up a bit, and you're not used to it," Heather said.

"Can we please stop talking about this?" Vivien begged. "I want to know what you meant when you said you were sure we were due for more superpowers. Did you talk to Julia's spirit? Did she say something about our gifts?"

"No. It was just a feeling, or maybe a worry." Heather looked into the bag. "My goodness, Viv, seriously how much food did you order?"

Vivien shrugged. "They reheat well and the fridge was empty."

"You eat like a frat boy," Heather pulled food

from the bag and laid the individually wrapped items on the table. Vivien ignored the remark.

"A month ago, I would have been all for more superpowers, but right now I'm not sure I can handle anything else. My empathic abilities have flared up like a psychic rash. They're all over the place. I'm sensing everything." Vivien unwrapped the end of a taco and took a bite.

The flour shell was lightly fried and the inside was filled with seasoned beef, peas, potatoes, cheese, and salsa. So simple, and so freaking good. She gave a light moan of appreciation.

Good food. Great friends. What else was there in life? Vivien counted herself very blessed.

"Lorna? Anything new happen to you?" Heather asked.

"I haven't used my healing power," Lorna said. "It feels a little too much like playing God. I shouldn't be the one to decide who deserves to be healed and who deserves to be injured.

"I disagree," Vivien said, not for the first time in counter to Lorna's thinking. "I think you're the perfect person. It's why you have the gift. If there were an injured child and a serial killer, I think you'd know what to do."

"Life choices are rarely that black-and-white, but

yes," Lorna agreed, "if it comes down to a child and a serial killer, I'll make a choice."

"What about your finding power?" Heather asked.

"There has been little need for it," Lorna admitted. "Though, I was able to find Vivien's lost earring the other morning, so you know, I'm practically a private detective."

"There's a cool job idea." Vivien clapped her hands in excitement. "We can start a detective agency. Oh, or bounty hunters."

"I have a job," Lorna denied, choosing a couple of the tamales. She leaned on her uninjured hip. "Managing the haunted theater is excitement enough. I don't want to limp after some criminal."

"What did you mean by psychic rash?" Heather studied her as if she could see some manifestation on Vivien's skin.

"It's nothing." Vivien waved her hand in dismissal. "I'm being dramatic."

"It's not nothing. Remember, we all agreed we have to talk about these things." Heather touched the bag beside her on the couch and patted it. "Or else I will burn this so no one ever finds it again. If we're going to meddle in the otherworldly, we need to talk to each other. Grandma Julia said we all came together to help each other heal. I think after what happened to Lorna, we all know that isn't just some easy prospect. I'm willing to travel this path with you, but we have to be smart and open. No secrets."

"My senses are in overdrive," Vivien explained. "I see a guy in a passing car, and I know he only dates redheads and hates the rain. I now know Mr. Pete down at the grocery store will only wear blue underwear because his wife said she liked the color once when they were dating. Melba likes to reenact scenes from paranormal romance novels at night when she closes up the bookstore in a one-woman show. She draws vampire bites on her neck with red lipstick. Ace the cat watches the performances."

"That's oddly specific." Heather appeared skeptical, which hurt a little since Heather was the only one who'd ever believed her about her gifts when they were younger. Vivien's grandmother had raised her not to feel shame about her gifts. That hadn't meant it was easy to be laughed at by the other children in school or treated like a kook as an adult.

"It's so random," Vivien groaned. "And it's blocking the things that I *should* see. I had no idea what was coming at the law office today, but I knew Mrs. Cameron planned on tuna noodle casserole for lunch and was rejected for a pet adoption some years back. In the elevator, I was so obsessed with telling some woman not to date a potential jerk that I walked right into..."

"Into?" Lorna prompted.

"Never mind," Vivien dismissed.

"Viv," Heather demanded.

"I walked right into giving Troy a ride home." She rubbed her temples as frustration seeped through her. She couldn't want Troy. He was all wrong for her. "Then, on the drive, I completely missed that he was about to ask me out and didn't deflect the question in time. I said all the wrong things. He probably thinks I was flirting with him. Which I wasn't. And I know he thinks I'm an imbecile. I just can't... I can't get... The words are just all jumbled when I am around him. It's like some invisible force grabs my throat and messes with my brain."

"I think that means you like him," Heather said.

"I don't want that kind of complication," Vivien said, and she meant it. Her life was decent, and she was secure in her decisions. "I like one-night stands that mean nothing. I get sex, and they get to go home to Omaha or wherever."

Heather nodded. "So that's what's bothering you. A man asked you out and you didn't see it coming in time to scare him away. Didn't you mention to me when he moved in that the new neighbor was a professor of some sort? So he's older, smart, has a job, and by all accounts is a hottie. This guy threw you for a loop."

"I should have bought more tacos," Vivien muttered, grabbing another one before she'd even finished the one she was on. She stuffed her mouth to keep from answering Heather's inquiry.

"Yeah, because two-four-six," Heather chuckled as she pretended to count, "forty isn't enough."

"These *are* fantastic," Lorna agreed with a nod.

"Try this one." Vivien lifted one of the beef tacos toward Lorna.

"You're avoiding the subject," Heather said.

"Yes, I am. I'm done talking about it," Vivien said. "What about you? Anything new happen?"

Heather sighed, and it was her turn to look dismissive of the conversation.

"What?" Lorna and Vivien asked in unison.

"The spirits are becoming clearer, and louder," Heather answered. "Which means the headaches are getting worse."

"Can you ignore them?" Lorna asked.

"If I ignore the active hauntings, I get a headache. If I try to listen, I get a headache. If they see me looking in their direction, they sometimes try to

follow which means the headache won't go away."
Heather shrugged. "That's it. Nothing new. I've been
dealing with ghosts my whole life."

"I can sense that there is more to it. The talking-
about-it thing goes all ways. You need to tell us what
you're going through." Lorna placed a hand on
Heather's arm. Her hair lifted off her shoulders at the
contact. She took a deep breath and looked at Vivien.

Vivien leaned forward to touch Heather. The
mere brush of skin to skin caused a zap of static electricity and they were able to share each other's
emotions. This happened whenever they made phys-
ical contact. Their souls connected. She instantly felt
the electrical charge flowing through her. Typically,
with Heather, there was an underlying sadness she'd
carried since losing her son. That emotion was still
there, but with it came a feeling of dread.

"You're feeling the spirits more," Vivien said,
understanding where the emotion was coming from.

Heather looked at Vivien's hand on her arm. She
arched a brow. "You're terrified because you are
attracted to Troy, much more than you let on."

Vivien snatched her hand back. For a moment,
she'd forgotten that the emotional sharing went both
ways.

"It's not true, you know," Heather insisted.

"You're not betraying Sam by liking someone else. It's been twenty years. I knew Sam. He loved you. He would want you to find happiness. He would have been pissed that you married Rex because he never made you happy."

"I'll be watching you. Save your heart for me. It's mine."

Vivien wasn't so sure about that. Sam's last words had not faded with time. He didn't want her to find someone else, because he knew there could be no one else for her. She wasn't one of the lucky women in her family.

"I still feel him around me," Vivien said. "I know you never see him, but I feel him sometimes. It's like a presence watching me from the foot of my bed while I sleep. Or maybe it's just a wish, not a haunting."

Vivien looked at the bag on the couch. Inside was her key to seeing Sam again. The book had belonged to Julia.

What if their powers could do more than summon his spirit?

What if they could bring him back?

What if she didn't have to be one of the unlucky ones?

What if she could regain her true love?

Vivien would never say those thoughts out loud, not even to the two people she trusted most in the world. Lorna had wanted to see her ex-husband to ask why he'd betrayed her. She had wanted to use the book of séances to find answers. They'd successfully contacted Glenn, and Lorna received the closure she needed. Heather was still trying to get the courage to talk to the spirit of her son, but when she was ready, they'd help her do whatever she needed to do.

If they could bring Sam back, what was to say they couldn't do the same for Heather's son? Vivien would never mention such a thing for fear it would give Heather false hope, but if she proved it could be done then Heather would know it was possible.

"If you're not ready, we don't have to do this," Heather said.

"No, I want to séance him tonight. If Sam has changed his mind and wants me to move on, then he can tell me that himself," Vivien said.

Lorna's hand was still on Heather as if it was taking her longer to decipher what she was sensing. She slowly let go and reached to smooth down her statically charged hair. "Are you picking up the ghosts' emotions? Is that what's new? Is that where all that apprehension you're feeling is coming from?"

"Some. There are more of them, but many seem

to be residual hauntings, unaware of anything around them. The residual spirits are easier to be around, but they're sad to watch. They just loop short scenes from their lives. It's either from something they often did, like one of my properties has a maid who hangs laundry on a clothesline for about a minute in the afternoons." Heather busied herself pulling more food items from the bag and setting them on the coffee table.

"What else?" Vivien prompted.

"It's not just mundane tasks like the laundry. It can be something that has left an emotional imprint like a man silently shouting from a window at a dilapidated building and banging his hands on the glass that's no longer there. Those are the hardest to see. I don't think they died easily." Heather picked at her taco, bringing torn pieces of the shell to her mouth. "A contractor I work with caught me talking to one. The ghost had been wearing work clothes and appeared completely solid. I thought he was a new guy until he walked through a wall that used to have a doorway. I looked like the crazy lady holding a conversation with herself."

"I wish there were a way we could know they were around, not that I think seeing them every-where would be better." Lorna hugged her arms around herself and glanced over the room. Vivien couldn't blame her for being apprehensive. Anyone would be on edge after an invisible demon had kicked the crap out of them.

"Thankfully, there are none in here," Heather assured her. "Just being here with you two, I'm already feeling better."

"We should eat," Lorna said. "We'll need our energy if we're going to séance Sam tonight."

CHAPTER FOUR

HEATHER STACKED empty wrappers on her plate and handed them to Vivien as they cleaned up their dinner mess. However, several uneaten items were still stacked on the coffee table and in the bag. Vivien left them where they were in case someone wanted to pick at the food later.

After Vivien dropped the trash off in the kitchen, she came back to find Heather had the messenger bag on her lap and was in the process of pulling Julia's séancing book from within.

The padded cover had been embossed with a circle and included symbols that matched their three rings. Whoever had made the book had taken a lot of time and care on its creation. Julia had safeguarded the book beneath the stage at Warrick theater, where she used to hold séances for the public.

To most people in town, famous Medium Julia Warrick was a colorful page of local history. No one admitted that they believed she could actually speak to the dead. Like many mediums during the spiritualist movement of the late-nineteenth and early-twentieth centuries, she was thought to be somewhat of a fraud at worst and a kook at best.

The book wasn't just one of Heather's family heirlooms. It was important. It was *magic*. It contained all the secrets Julia had deemed necessary enough to write down for future generations.

"I was reading some of the recipes and looking up ingredients online. I think there are ways to protect ourselves." Heather opened the cover to the title page that read *"Warrick"* in calligraphy. The entire book had been written by hand, which made some of the entries harder to read. However, it also added to the secrecy of its contents. Some of the pages had decorative borders along the edges, some whimsical vines, others art deco lines. Julia had been a fan of art deco if the style of the theater was any indication.

Heather turned the thick pages several at a time. The first section was lists of séances that Julia had done in the 1920s and '30s, which said things like, *"December 9, 1928, Fiona O'Leary, six dollars to contact three-year-old daughter Mirabella. Not earthbound,"* and, *"Jane Benoit, three dollars to contact mother, Josephine. Hateful woman. Ex.,"* and, *"So-and-so traded a chicken to contact Joe to find out where he hid his mother's brooch."*

They found out the hard way that Ex. stood for exorcism. It was a clean-up step they'd forgotten to take when contacting Lorna's dead husband, Glenn. Apparently, certain cranky spirits could bring other demonic figures through the veil with them.

In many ways, the book represented utter sadness. It listed name after name of grieving people trying to find answers from the other side. Vivien didn't know how Julia had done what she did. Vivien couldn't imagine absorbing so much grief from those around her.

Heather continued turning the pages. The ring vibrated on Vivien's finger, sending a small current up her arm. Heather stopped when she found the drawing of a candle.

"Here." Heather pointed at a candle-making recipe. "I mean, yes, some of my information came from the internet, so we take it with a grain of salt because not everyone agrees on everything, but I think this light blue candle is for amplifying our message to the dead. We were just lighting whatever was around, and I think we have to give the candle intention? I'm still figuring it all out. Then there are these. They are anointed in basil oil. Basil, coconut, garlic, they're all traditionally used for protection. Blueberries are to help against psychic attacks. I don't know if we eat them or smell them or what."

"I vote eat," Lorna said. "In pie form."

"I second that," Vivien added, grinning.

"I was going to say blueberry vodka form." Heather chuckled.

"Oh, no, no drinks tonight. We all agreed," Lorna said. "Though I would enjoy a red wine about right now." Just as Vivien was about to get up to grab a bottle, she added, "Kidding. Kidding. We're being good. No drunk séancing any demons tonight."

"So what are you saying? We need to go get candle-making supplies now?" Vivien asked.

"Could be a fun project," Lorna said. Of course, Lorna also liked to cook, so she *would* think boiling candle wax sounded fun. For Vivien, it seemed like it would be cool once or twice, but she'd grow bored eventually.

"We could," Heather said, "but luckily we have something Julia didn't. Overnight shipping."

Heather reached into her bag and pulled out blue candles. She placed them on the table. "I intend for these to help us communicate with the dead better."

Vivien nodded. "Okay. I intend the same."

"Me too," Lorna said.

Heather nodded, though it was clear they weren't exactly sure of what they were doing, or if just stating an intention would even work. She then took out a bundle of herbs.

"Smudging seems pretty straightforward. We should start doing it at least once a month, maybe once a week." Heather set the smudging sticks on the table next to the candles. "We light these sticks of sage and lavender, then bring the smoke around each room counterclockwise along the walls and cast out negative energy. When we're done, we smother the ends in sand." She took out a bag of sand and a bowl. "I tried it at the theater earlier. I know it sounds odd, but I think it helped lighten the area of negative energy."

"You did this alone? At the theater?" Lorna frowned. She lifted her thigh and adjusted her sore hip.

"I'm with Lorna on this one. We shouldn't do anything like this alone," Vivien said.

"I thought it was worth a try. I can't keep canceling all the shows." Heather set the bowl and bag of sand on the table. "I want it to be safe when people return. And William was with me. He's trying to learn about this stuff too. He wants to be supportive."

Vivien knew Heather was frightened for the safety of theater patrons and that she also needed the theater to bring in business in order to pay the property taxes on her inheritance.

Vivien nodded. "Okay. Good. I'm glad your brother was there with you."

William had spent most of his life denying his family's ability to see ghosts, so supporting them in their new hobby was an enormous step for him.

"Is that what he went to help you with earlier?" Lorna asked. "He mentioned meeting you at the theater. I thought it had to do with shoring up the stage."

They'd found the book by tripping a hidden lever that caused the stage floor to drop. By all rights, there should have been a hole in the floor, but somehow the trap door reversed itself, and they hadn't been able to get back inside—not that they needed to. The lever no longer worked.

"We've looked at it, but I think the stage floor will

hold," Heather said. "The only thing left under there besides some old ropes and broken pullies is Julia's altar. I think it was more of a set prop than anything. There are no drawings of it in the book to make me think it is important."

"I think I'm ready to go back to work," Lorna said. "I can't keep lying around here all day long. Besides, I can't let you pay me for doing nothing. You forgot to turn off the autopay into my bank account this week. Plus, I shudder to think what my hospital bill will look like when it comes."

Heather looked like she might protest, but then said, "I'll make you a deal. I'll let you come back to work if you let us take some of that pain away from you so you *can* work."

Vivien nodded. "Yep. I agree."

"But—" Lorna began to protest.

"No more buts. I can't stand to see you sitting sideways like that any longer." Vivien stood. She walked toward the couch and kneeled in front of Lorna. She grabbed Lorna's hand and pulled it to rest against her own hip. "Do it."

Lorna tried to pull her hand away from Vivien, but Vivien held on tight. Lorna bit the corner of her lip and closed her eyes. Vivien's thigh tingled and ached where Lorna touched her. Lorna didn't transfer much, but the woman gave a small sigh as the tingling sensation stopped.

"Was that too much?" Lorna asked.

Vivien rubbed her hip. It felt like a sore muscle from working out too hard. "It's fine."

"Okay, now me," Heather said. She angled her butt toward Lorna. When Lorna hesitated, she teased, "I don't back this hiney up for just anyone. Lay it on me."

Lorna laughed and gave Heather's hip a light smack. Then, with a deep breath as if steadying herself, she put her hand on Heather and closed her eyes. Vivien watched Heather squint as the pain transferred into her. It wasn't long before Lorna lifted her hand.

Heather shifted her weight on the couch. "That's not too bad."

"Can you sit up now?" Vivien asked.

Lorna leaned to the side, gave a small moan, and smiled. "Omigod, I can't believe how much that helped. Thank you."

Lorna wiggled back and forth on the cushion as if testing her healed hip.

"You should have done it days ago," Heather said. "Next time listen to us."

"Two days ago it hurt too badly," Lorna denied. "I couldn't share that level of—"

"My point exactly," Heather countered. "What are friends for if not to help carry the load. We were all there when we brought that dogface demon into our world. There is no reason why you are the only one who has to suffer because of it."

They'd made the argument before. Lorna had refused to listen.

"What I should have done is take you with me to see Rex," Vivien said, as the idea occurred to her. She went back to her seat. The hip was sore, but she wouldn't let Lorna see that it bothered her. "You can transfer all the suffering you want to that giant asshole."

"Here, eat your feelings," Heather instructed, nudging a wrapped burrito toward Vivien.

Vivien groaned and shook her head. "I can't eat anymore. Fine, I concede. I might have over-ordered."

"Ya think?" Heather chuckled. "Listen, you need to push Rex out of your thoughts. What he did to you sucked, and it's over now. You don't need him. You don't need his money. What happens going forward with the alimony will only change your life by small degrees. Don't forget why we're here. Tonight is about you finding closure with Sam."

Julia had told Heather that was why the three of them were brought together—to help each other heal their pain. Vivien nodded, not correcting Heather's stated intention.

"Save your heart for me. It's mine."

She remembered every detail of Sam's last day. If she let it, the pain would roll through her. This was more than trying to find closure about Sam's death. She wanted to find a way to get him back. For good. Sam was nothing like Glenn. There should be no risk of demons and ill-will. Sam had been a decent man and a great husband. He'd let nothing hurt them. "You're right. Thank you for the reminder."

"So, if you smudged the theater for ghosts, did that make Julia go away too?" Lorna asked, rolling a sage and lavender smudging stick between her hands before bringing it to her face to smell the fragrant bundle.

"No. She's not negative energy. I saw her watching me when I was going through. I can't be sure, but I think she was smiling and nodding," Heather answered. "It's strange. She hasn't been as vocal lately, but the others are. I'm hoping smudging scared off any leftover negative energy, and she'll start talking again. I'd give anything for a straight answer. Her telling us that we're brought together to help us heal from our past pains without telling us *how* we're supposed to do that is so vague it's annoying. Even if she were talking to me right now, I'm not sure it would matter. Spirits rarely give a straightforward answer about anything. Normally they're too confused."

"We're doing the right thing," Vivien said. She leaned to the side and artfully tried to stretch her sore hip without being obvious about it. "This is our path. I feel it. We are meant to learn how to wield this magic."

That wasn't exactly true. She couldn't be sure if she felt this way because it was what they were supposed to be doing or because she wanted it to be what they were meant to be doing. All she knew was that the ache inside her had a name.

Sam.

"Save your heart for me. It's mine."

She needed to see Sam. For twenty years she'd carried that name in her heart, and now she had the chance to hear him and see him, hopefully touch him. It had taken her days of begging to talk her friends into trying again. Now that she had them here, she would not let them talk themselves out of it.

She needed this to work.

Heather stood. "Okay, let's do this then. I'll grab the card table, and we'll set up in here. It seems as good of a place as any."

"What about the dining room?" Lorna asked.

"I think that table might be too big. It won't be conducive to holding hands, at least not comfortably," Heather said. "Is it still in the storage closet?"

Vivien nodded and Heather disappeared down the hallway.

Vivien hurried to her room to change out of the business suit. She'd been halfway into a dress when she remembered that in high school she'd been more of a beach bum than a beauty queen. Instead, she'd opted for khaki capris, a t-shirt, and a long sweater jacket. It was something Sam would have expected her to wear.

When she returned to the living room, her friends had set up a séance area on the folding table. The directions illustrated in the book were simple. They placed the book in the middle of the table and then set the candles around it—blue for clarity according to the candle-making instructions.

The illustration showed them placing their hands with the forefinger rings on the book to form a triangle, but already they found holding hands connected them better. Heather had wrote out what they should say from the multiple examples in the book. That way they'd all be on the same page when it came time to call Sam.

The light from the window had darkened as evening turned to night. Vivien closed the curtains, not wanting anyone peeking in on what they were doing. Her street did not get a lot of traffic this time of night, but the occasional tourist did try to sneak past her lawn to the beach.

Vivien's bare toes curled against the carpet. She felt almost giddy with excitement. The first time they'd tried a séance, she'd been too drunk to form a coherent thought. This time would be different. This time she'd get Sam to show himself.

"I think I ate too much," Lorna said, rubbing her stomach.

Vivien knew it wasn't the tacos. Lorna eyed the book nervously. They'd been discussing this for nearly two weeks, but this was the first time they were going to summon a spirit since the attack. It was clearly a challenging prospect for her friend.

"We don't have to do this." Heather reached for Lorna's hand, hesitated, and then pulled away without touching her. The friendly gesture of reaching out was automatic, but they were getting better at catching themselves before making contact. There were very little secrets amongst the three of them.

Vivien was sure when the novelty of the experience wore off, it would become annoying. She didn't want them, even as her friends, knowing what she felt every second of the day. Yeah, she usually would tell them everything anyway, but sometimes a woman needed to process what she was feeling before others weighed in—like with Troy. She didn't know why the new neighbor flustered her as much as he did.

However, it wasn't lost on Vivien that usually it was she who knew what everyone else was thinking even if they didn't want her to. It was a lot different being on the other side of the experience.

Tonight was not the night to try to figure that out. Tonight was about Sam.

"Lorna? Just say the word and we'll stop," Heather asserted.

Vivien's breath caught, and she stiffened, waiting for Lorna's response. Lorna could stop the night's events with one word—any of them could for any reason. If Lorna said no, then Vivien would respect her wishes.

Vivien felt tears threatening her eyes, and she

forced them back. She held still. Time felt like it slowed as she waited for the answer. She didn't want to manipulate Lorna with her pain, but she wanted this so badly.

Sam.

The name whispered through her thoughts like a plea to the universe.

Sam.

Please, Sam.

Lorna's eyes met hers, and Vivien knew the woman understood. "I'm all right. We'll be smarter this time. No demons. Just Sam."

Sam.

Vivien tried to smile, but the gesture was weak. She looked at the book. If this worked, Sam would be standing in front of her on the book as it rested on the card table in the middle of her living room.

"Light the candles," Lorna said. "Let's do this."

Heather went to the messenger bag on the couch and pulled out a candle lighter. She pressed the trigger a couple of times before a flame erupted from the tip. She drew the flame to the first candlewick and whispered, "Our intent is to talk to Sam Stone."

As if some mystical force answered her words, the remaining candles in the room lit before Heather could pull the lighter away from the first one. Not only was it the four on the table, but the decorative candles Vivien had placed around the room. She even saw a soft glow coming from the kitchen pass-through.

The overhead lights flickered. Vivien expected that to happen, as it had happened each time they tried this.

"I wonder what it is about stirring spirits that cause them to drain power from everything," Lorna said, looking at the now dark overhead lights.

"They need the energy to manifest themselves," Heather said.

"What do you think ghosts used before electricity?" Vivien wondered.

"People?" Heather supposed. She laid the pieces of paper on the table so everyone could read the spell at the same time during the ceremony. "Powerful emotions?"

"Maybe that's why they had group séances. Groups of people in a heightened state might be enough to fuel an entity," Lorna said.

Vivien placed her hands on the card table and slid them toward her friends. If heightened emotion is all it took, then she had enough this evening to bring back Sam fifty times. "I'm ready."

Heather and Lorna shared a look. Lorna nodded.

They all three joined hands, forming a circle around the book. The curtains fluttered, and the blinds made a rattling noise the moment they made contact. Vivien felt the energy flooding through her body. Hair lifted from her shoulders, tingling as the current flowed through her. She saw the same effect on Heather and Lorna. Heather gave her an encouraging smile. Lorna's lips were pressed tightly together.

Vivien felt Lorna's apprehension, but also her determination. Lorna had become accustomed to putting her own wishes and feelings aside for others. She'd done it her entire adult life—as a wife to Glenn and as a mother of three. She was probably the most giving person Vivien had ever met.

From Heather, Vivien detected the same hard knot of pain that was always there since the death of her son. It lingered in the background of everything Heather did. It had become a permanent fixture, and Vivien wasn't sure there would ever be a way to get rid of it.

In truth, Heather wouldn't want the pain to go away. That pain was her child. There was nothing that could compare to such a loss.

Vivien glanced down at the piece of paper. She felt her quickening heartbeat in her throat and chest.

The word judge caught her attention. "I don't want to judge Sam."

"It's the séance from the book that fits the closest, and it worked with Glenn. I thought maybe it was best we didn't stray too far from Julia's wording," Heather said. "And it's not like we're going to judge him harshly or anything. I don't think that matters."

Vivien nodded. "All right."

She wasn't sure if it was nerves or excitement that caused her to tremble. A sudden rush of questions flooded her. What would he think of her now? Would he think she was old? She didn't feel old in her forties, but what would she have thought about this age when she was twenty?

Would he remember their love?

Would he remember her?

She had no clue what the afterlife held. It might have felt like centuries to him.

What if he were haunting some other woman?

What if—?

"Vivien, stop," Heather said, squeezing her hand tight. "Take a breath. It's all right."

Vivien blinked. She was breathing hard, and her heart pounded.

"We can stop whenever you want," Lorna said.

"But it helped me to see Glenn. It helped to say goodbye to him. Let us help you do the same."

Vivien didn't want to say goodbye to Sam. She wanted him back. If magic was real, then why couldn't magic give her back the love of her life?

Before the other two could sense her secret wish and decide to stop, Vivien looked down at the paper and began to read aloud, "We open the door—"

Lorna and Heather instantly joined her.

"—between two worlds to call forth the spirit of Sam Stone. Come back from the grave so that we may hear. Come back from the grave and show yourself to us so that all may see. Come back from the grave and answer for what you have done so that you may be judged."

Small pinpoints of light moved over the book. This was how it had started when they'd summoned Glenn. First the light would grow, then his feet would appear standing on the book. His ghost body had absorbed the light from the candles, and it became trapped inside his translucent form to illuminate his shape. She watched, waiting, her breath coming in ragged, audible pants. The lights grew brighter.

First the light. Then the feet.

Come on, Sam.

The lights dimmed and faded like cooling ash. Sam wasn't there.

"No," Vivien gasped, jumping up a little in her seat as she willed the lights to come back.

The room darkened, and only the candles flickered.

"We open the door between two worlds," Vivien said, the words rushed, "to call forth the spirit of Sam Stone."

The flames sputtered and then burned low. She felt energy surging through her, flowing like a circuit from Lorna and into Heather. Why wasn't he appearing?

"We call forth..." Vivien tightened her hold on her friends' hands. "Sam? Are you there? Can you hear me? Sam, come back to me."

"We open," Lorna began, her voice sturdy. Heather instantly joined her, "the door between," which prompted Vivien to do the same, "two worlds to call forth the spirit of Sam Stone. Come back from the grave so that we may hear. Come back from the grave and show yourself to us so that all may see. Come back from the grave and answer for what you have done so that you may be judged."

The lights acted like they were trying to shine but kept fading.

"Come on, Sam," Heather whispered.

Lorna repeated the words, "We open the door between two worlds to call forth the spirit of Sam Stone. Come back from the grave so that we may hear. Come back..."

As her friend chanted, Vivien rocked back and forth in her chair. She couldn't hear Lorna's words so much as the tone of her voice. Vivien willed Sam to appear with every ounce of her being. The light formed a shape, only to fade, and then build, and then fade, build, fade.

Why?

"He's trying," Heather said, not sounding convinced. "Come on, Sam."

"...come back from the grave and show your-self..." Lorna continued to chant.

"Come back to me, Sam," Vivien ordered. "Come back to me, baby. Come back."

"...back from the grave and answer..." Lorna continued.

"Sam, come back to—" Vivien gasped.

The flames from the blue candles burst, as if catching invisible threads on fire. The four streams of light twisted around each other as they filled in the shape of muscular legs. The light continued to build, growing as legs turned into hips in shorts.

"...to call forth the spirit of Sam Stone..." Lorna's voice faded into the background.

"Sam?" Vivien watched the light, focusing intently on what it revealed. She tilted her head back.

The firelight diffused into the see-through figure. It transformed the color of his skin and clothing and shifted the shadows of a firm stomach and chest. In all honesty, twenty years had done a lot to fade the exact memory of Sam's body. She had pictures that served as a reminder, but it wasn't until the light revealed his beautiful face that she knew for sure it was him.

Her Sam.

"Sam," she whispered, feeling tears of joy threatening her eyes. "Sam, that's it. Come back to me."

His dark brown eyes met hers as he looked down at her. She held tight to her friends, afraid if she let go, he'd disappear even though she knew it wasn't like the old movies they'd seen. Once a spirit appeared, they didn't need to keep holding hands for the séance to continue.

That face.

That mouth.

Those eyes.

Vivien panted for breath, unable to form the

words she wanted to say. He was here. Finally. It was real.

Her lips parted. She gazed up at him, wishing his face was solid so she could reach for him, touch him, feel him.

His hand lifted, the fingers extending as if he would touch her.

"Hi," she managed to whisper. "You're here—"

Suddenly, Sam's jaw distended. His mouth distorted in a wide scream. The sound blasted her like a gust of wind. Her hair blew back from her face. She imagined she smelled him—the familiar hint of fresh ocean air. She heard items crashing around her living room. The force of the wind became painful, stinging her skin like it pelted her with sand.

Sam's body burst, and he released the flames.

Heat rolled over Vivien's face and chest. The sound of his scream died as his light faded. The blue candles remained burning as if nothing had happened.

"Sam?" Vivien's voice caught on a sob. Her skin stung.

"What did we do?" Lorna whispered. "What was that?"

Heather's hand slipped from Vivien's, and she flipped over the paper with the séance chant. Almost panicked, she read, "Spirit you have been found pure. We release you into the light. Go in peace and love."

The blessing was supposed to end the séance, but Vivien felt Lorna's fear through their connected fingers that it had come too late. When Glenn was sent to his afterlife, he'd gone like dying embers. Sam had exploded in heat and pain. The feel of it stuck to her skin, prickling her nerve endings.

"What did we do?" Lorna asked again. "What was that? I don't think that was supposed to happen. Did you feel—?"

"Shh," Heather shushed the woman as she came around the table to grab Vivien by the face. "Viv? Look at me. Are you all right? I need you to take a deep breath for me. Focus on my eyes. That's it. Focus on me."

Vivien tried to speak, but her chest squeezed and the pressure made it difficult.

A loud bang sounded on the door seconds before it crashed open. "Vivien?"

The sound of Troy's voice barely registered. Lorna's hand pulled out of her grasp. Heather's hands remained on her face, forcing Vivien to look at her.

"Are you all right? What happened? Is there

someone in the house?" Troy's questions flooded the room. "I heard a woman screaming."

"We were playing around, and we startled Vivien," Heather said, her eyes staying on Vivien's.

Vivien touched her lips. Had she screamed?

"So, you're..." Troy appeared in her peripheral. "She doesn't look all right. Maybe I should call an ambulance."

"Hey, Troy, right?" Lorna said, her tone calm. "Hi. I'm Lorna. I just moved in a few weeks ago. We haven't met yet. You know Viv, and this is Heather. An ambulance won't be necessary. You can put your phone away."

"Viv?" Heather's light brown eyes came more into focus as she drew an exaggerated breath trying to prompt Vivien to breathe. "That's right. Just like that."

"What happened in here?" Troy insisted.

Vivien finally managed a deep breath. She blinked, shaking the feeling of fear from her body. She pulled Heather's hands from her face.

"What?" Vivien forced herself to stand and turn around to look at him. "Don't like my decorating?"

"Uh?" Troy glanced at the floor.

The words had left her before she actually saw her living room. The gust of air had not only stunned her, but it had trashed her home. The vases had crashed into broken pieces. The Renaissance paintings of women had fallen off the walls. The uneaten Mexican food was on the floor.

"I'm sorry if we were too loud." Vivien smiled even though she felt weak. "You know how wild girls' night can get."

"Margaritas, whew," Heather added. "Straight to our heads."

"Yeah, sorry for the noise," Lorna said, not as convincing as the other two. "We'll try to keep it down."

"Uh, okay," Troy mumbled in disbelief. "I'm glad everything is..." He looked around. "Sorry for barging in like that."

"Hey, thanks for being concerned," Heather said, lifting her hand to usher him toward the front door as she stepped around the mess of food on the floor. "And it was very nice to meet you, Troy."

Vivien waited for the door to close before turning to stare at the book. She gave a weak laugh. "I guess Sam didn't like my decorating choices."

"Don't joke," Lorna said. "This is serious."

"Viv, are you all right?" Heather asked.

"Where did he go?" Vivien pointed toward the book as if doing so would make sense out of what happened. "Why were there flames this time? Do you think that means he's in hell?"

"Sam? No," Heather instantly denied. "He can't be in hell. That's not a place for a man like him."

"But I felt..." Vivien rubbed her arms through the sweater jacket. Her body ached. "I felt him pass through me. It hurt."

"Is that why you were screaming?" Lorna asked.

"Sam screamed. Not me," Vivien denied.

"No, sweetie, that was you," Heather stated.

Vivien shook her head in confusion. She'd seen him scream, saw the horror of his distended jaw.

"You're shaking like a leaf, Viv," Heather said. "Are you cold?"

"I don't think so," Vivien answered.

"I think you should lie down," Lorna insisted. "Heather, why don't you help her to her room? I'll clean up this mess."

Heather nodded. "Yeah, I think that's an excellent idea. Come on, hon. Let's get you into bed."

Vivien allowed Heather to lead her down the hall to her bedroom. She was grateful for the guidance.

"I don't think Troy will be asking me out again anytime soon," Vivien tried to joke, but her words did not have the teasing quality she'd hoped for.

"I think it was nice he tried to rescue you,"

Heather said. "Even though if I ever met a woman who didn't need to be rescued by a man, it's you."

They made it to her bedroom. Heather rushed a few feet ahead of her and pulled back the covers.

"Get in," Heather ordered.

Vivien obeyed, too shaken to protest. She lay on her side, drawing her legs toward her chest. Heather pulled the covers over her and pushed them around her body to tuck her in.

"That was Sam," Vivien said as Heather smoothed back her hair. "I smelled him. Did you smell him?"

"No, I saw him pass through you, though. Maybe that was his way of saying goodbye." She didn't sound convinced. "Spirits can't always communicate the way we expect them to."

"Do you think he was still confused because of how he died? With all that morphine in his system? He had a hard time talking at the end."

"I don't know." Heather moved around to the other side of the bed to lie next to her.

"I thought spirits were supposed to be cold. Sam was hot," Vivien insisted, rolling over to look at her friend. Heather had stayed on top of the covers.

"I honestly don't know what happened, but I promise you, we will figure it out. I have to believe we were brought together and given these abilities for a reason. Grandma Julia would not have sent us down this path if it were the wrong one." Heather smoothed back Vivien's hair and rested her hand on the side of her head. "Whatever it takes, I promise, you'll get your chance to tell him goodbye."

Vivien felt a hot tear slide along the side of her nose. "I miss him so much."

"I know, hon. I know." Heather brushed the tear away.

"Don't leave me. Stay here tonight. I don't want to be alone," Vivien whispered, closing her eyes. "I'm suddenly extremely tired."

Heather withdrew her hand. "I'm not going anywhere. I promise. I'll be right here."

CHAPTER FIVE

Vivien awoke from a deep sleep to the buzzing motion alarm on her cell phone. By the lack of light in her bedroom window, she could deduce that it was in the middle of the night. She automatically reached for her phone to dismiss the notification since it was most likely William sneaking in to see Lorna. Again. If these late-night visits kept up, she'd end up disabling the damned thing.

Vivien chuckled softly. It was rather sweet. William and Lorna were like two teenagers in love. If he wanted to sneak in her window, so be it. Metaphorically speaking, of course. She didn't actually want him climbing through the windows.

The sound of soft breathing caused her to lift her phone higher in confusion. She used the light from the screen to see who was next to her. Heather's arm sprawled over her head, and she mumbled as the light hit her face. She still wore her jeans and flannel, but she'd kicked off her shoes. Vivien instantly lowered the light to let her friend sleep.

This wasn't the first time Heather had crashed at her house, but seeing her reminded Vivien of the evening before. They'd tried to contact Sam. The encounter had left her weak, and she barely remembered Heather walking her to the bed.

Vivien looked at her phone. She didn't recall putting it on the charger, but then automatically sensed that Lorna, in her thoughtfulness, had done it for her. She turned the phone in her hand. She usually didn't pick up intense psychic impressions from objects.

Worse than the exhaustion were the feelings of fear and sadness that had settled into her chest. The emotions weighed on her heart and stomach, and each breath felt labored.

The ghost had been Sam. She'd seen his face, however briefly. He'd looked like he had before cancer ate away at him. She'd smelled the ocean on him when he'd passed over her. He'd always loved being near the water. It was one of the reasons she'd never moved away from the ocean. She felt him in the waves.

Vivien couldn't help but think she'd fucked things up royally. Heather was right. There was no way a guy like Sam was in hell. So whatever pain he suffered had to be because they'd brought him back. Had they yanked him out of heaven? Was there even such a place?

Vivien didn't consider herself super religious, but she believed there was more beyond this life. She liked to think that place was heaven. If there could be hell, there had to be a heaven.

Maybe the difference between Glenn's return and Sam's was time. Glenn had only been dead for three years. She lost Sam twenty years ago. But that made little sense. Grandma Julia showed herself to Heather and she'd been gone a long time.

Vivien slid out of bed, moving slowly as not to jar the mattress and wake her friend. She needed a moment alone. On habit, she took her cell phone with her. She pushed the notification for the motion alarm. The camera feed tried to load. She carried it with her as she walked.

Vivien peeked into the hall, looking for William. All was quiet. She made her way toward the kitchen. She vaguely remembered Lorna saying she would pick up the mess in the living room. A broken frame lay on the coffee table, and her vases were missing. She found she didn't really care that they were broken. The empty space looked better.

Vivien had slept in her clothes, so she thought nothing of slipping into the pair of sandals she kept by the kitchen door leading to the backyard. Trash bags sat on the kitchen floor. She nudged them with her foot, hearing the light clank of broken ceramics. Poor Lorna probably couldn't have gotten the bags down the steps with her sore hip.

Vivien slid her cell phone into her pocket. The video clip had yet to load. Her muscle was still sore where Lorna had shared her pain, but it wasn't anything to cry over. She unlocked the door and lifted the trash bags to carry them to the bins.

The fresh night air welcomed her, and she took a deep breath. She loved walking around at night. Freewild Cove was a relatively safe town. Yes, there were some tourist-related crimes, but they mostly were drunk and disorderly charges. Sometimes there was vandalism and destruction of property, but again, usually alcohol and vacationers were involved.

Her phone buzzed as she moved past the motion sensor camera. She automatically glanced up and smiled as she walked across the yard to the bins by the back gate. It was pointless since only she would see the recordings.

Well, her and any internet hackers who had a fondness for backyards.

Dropping the bags in the bin, she pulled the phone from her pocket and looked at the screen. She stopped the recording of herself and started to close the app when she noticed the earlier footage had finally loaded. A strange blue glow on the still frame caught her attention.

Vivien played the video clip. It was the time stamp that would have woken her up. A light moved across her lawn from the house toward the back gate. At first she thought it was a lens flare, but the light paused and a figure seemed to turn, showing what looked like two arms lifting ever so slightly before again moving toward the fence. The gate did not open, but the light passed through it and then disappeared.

Vivien glanced from her phone to the gate. Nothing was there. A chill worked over her. She peered over the backyard. As far as she could tell, there was nothing in the shadows.

She watched the video again. It definitely looked like an entity walked across the lawn. Her hands shook, and she again glanced around. The night was quiet except for the sound of the breeze in the trees and the distant rhythm of waves.

Vivien couldn't bring herself to move. She felt as if she were being watched. The house stood dark and still against the sky, and the moon hid behind the clouds. Her gaze went to the security camera.

Her hand shook as she brought up the video clip of her walking across the lawn with the trash bags. Her body was darker compared to the other one. She watched as she turned to smile up at the camera.

On the clip, a light crept across the lawn toward her from the gate.

Vivien gasped and again looked around before turning back to the clip. The figure had approached her, but at the time she hadn't seen or felt anything. A hand reached for the back of her head as she continued to walk toward the bins. It had followed her. The clip ended where she had turned the recording off.

Vivien took a deep breath, unsure of what to do. She wished Heather and Lorna were with her. Their presence would comfort her and calm her fears.

"Is someone there?" Vivien called softly. "Hello?"

The wind stirred, but she didn't feel anything out of the ordinary.

Vivien lifted her phone, this time turning on the camera app so she could look with the device. The image of the dark yard passed over the screen. She turned the phone slowly along the lawn, from the gate toward the house, and then back again. She took small steps toward the house when she saw the path was clear.

Just as she was about to relax, the blue figure returned, standing several feet away. Vivien inhaled sharply and held the phone at arm's length. She glanced at the figure on the screen and then at the empty yard. What was on the electronic device was not appearing to the naked eye. It moved toward her, slowly, before turning toward the gate. It again walked through the fence.

Was this one of those residual hauntings Heather had talked about? Some spirit caught in a loop, doomed to spend eternity walking across her lawn to the back fence?

The blue entity stopped on the other side and stood. Vivien waited, watching intently. The image took on more of a shape. An arm lifted as if beckoning her to follow.

She again glanced to where the spirit stood, not seeing it without the aid of the camera phone. "Sam? Is that you?"

She wanted it to be true. She needed it to be him.

Vivien glanced toward the house, wondering if she should tell someone she was going down to the beach. But what if the entity went away when she ran inside? Besides, Lorna was recovering, and Heather was sleeping. If they needed her all they had to do was call her phone.

Vivien took small, hesitant steps as she followed the being. She unlatched the gate with one hand and pushed it open. The entity moved farther away along the path that led toward the beach and then stopped as if waiting.

Residual hauntings weren't aware of their surroundings. This ghost wanted her to follow it. That meant it had to be intelligent. It was communicating with her.

Him, not *it*. This had to be Sam. They'd summoned his spirit just hours before, and the odds of someone else coming to visit her were unlikely.

Or so she wanted to tell herself.

She refused to think about the demon that had come when they called Glenn. This wasn't the same thing. The demon had been raw hate and had attacked Lorna. This spirit wasn't threatening or attacking.

Vivien left the yard and moved down the familiar

path toward the beach. She passed between a couple of her neighbors' houses, using the phone to track the spirit. If this were Sam, she had no reason to be frightened.

A few trees had been planted for privacy, but they soon gave way to tall grass and then a sandy incline. The view opened up. A weathered picket fence had been beaten by the sun and buried by sand. It now poked out of the ground at an odd angle. She knew there were wooden planks on the ground that someone had tried to make a walkway with, but without constant sweeping they had been submerged. A wooden walkover would have been more prudent, but the neighbors couldn't get on the same page as to who would pay for the upgrade.

"What are you trying to show me?" she asked, not receiving an answer. Now that she was in the open, the breeze from the water caused her to shiver, and she grabbed the long sweater with one hand to hold it closed. "The ocean?"

They had spent a lot of time on the beach together. Was he trying to remind her of that?

The figure turned and motioned that she was to continue with him. Vivien's heart pounded, and she knew she should stop and think about what she was doing, but she wasn't scared. She was excited. Sam would never hurt her. This was what she wanted—to be with him at all costs, to see him.

The sand became deeper, and the undulating water louder. The beach curved, and she knew during the day she'd see across to the distant shore, but at night it blended with the water.

Her open-toe sandals allowed sand to work its way beneath her feet, and the gritty texture made it uncomfortable to walk. She didn't care as she lifted and shook her foot a little with each step. Her toe bumped into a hard object, and she stumbled. Typically, she'd stop and pick up the empty bottles people had left behind, but she didn't want to take her eyes off the phone screen.

The light glided instead of walked, leaving no impression in the sand. The occasional lift of an arm and the blurry impression of a head was the only indication the spirit was human—or had once been human. It did not deviate from its path toward the water.

As dry sand turned to wet, the ground became firm and more comfortable to walk on. The spirit continued toward the water. Vivien stopped.

"I'm not going in there," she said. "It's too cold to go swimming."

She glanced both along the beach to a distant

gathering. A bonfire had been lit below the high tide line but far enough away from the vegetation to be legal. She detected tiny figures running around just as she and Sam used to do. That was where he should be trying to lead her if he wanted her to remember their past, not into the ocean.

When she turned back to her phone, she saw that the figure was standing in the water. She crept closer. Cold lapped against her feet.

"I don't understand," Vivien called out to the ghost, dropping her phone hand slightly so she could talk toward the empty water. "I can't go in there with you."

When she lifted her phone hand, the figure had moved. It now stood close to the screen. She gasped and stumbled back. The image of a face tried to make itself known, the blue light shadowing in what could have been eye sockets and a nose before blurring once more.

"Sam?" Vivien asked, her body shaking from the freezing water. "Is that you? Can you please give me a sign if—"

Before she could finish the question, the spirit reached for her. She felt her shoulder tingle as if it made contact. The sensation took her by surprise, traveling down her arm so that the phone slipped from her fingers. She heard it thud but couldn't move to pick it up.

The tingling worked its way down to her left foot. She took a step forward, the movement stilted. It wasn't that she tried to walk, but more like her nerves jerked, and she was compelled to move. The tingling spread to her right foot. She took another stiff step forward. The sensation overtook her body. Her left leg stumbled toward the water, her toes dragging as her sandal caught on the ground, and then the right foot did the same. Waves lapped up against her ankles.

"Sam?" Vivien whispered, wanting to hear his voice. Her lids became heavy as a haze overtook her thoughts. She was compelled to take another step, not caring that it was too cold.

"Vivien?" The sound of her name was distant, faint, and she couldn't make out who said it through the fog in her brain.

"Sam?" she mumbled. "Is that you? I hear you. Talk to me."

She took a fumbling step, then another. The tingling numbed her to the cold, and it no longer stung. Low strains of music whispered their way into her thoughts. The guitar, just like Sam used to play for her on nights just like this. Her vision blurred.

"Save your heart for me. It's mine."

Sam.

She was with Sam.

She took another step. The water became almost warm now as she adjusted to the temperature. It came to her knees and then her thighs. It wet her long sweater jacket and weighed the ends down. The surface of the water kissed her hands, and she swung her arms to help leverage her movements. Water engulfed her hips and made it hard to step forward as the current lifted her from the ground. Her sandals slipped from her feet.

"Vivien!"

The sound was still distant, but she knew it was a man's voice. Was Sam calling her to him? Heather said spirits could be difficult to hear, often sounding like they were underwater or far away.

Without the phone, she couldn't see him, but she felt like he held her arm and led her forward. The current again lifted her from the ocean floor, moving her in little hops wherever it wanted. She went deeper.

The water hit her face and shoulders, and she coughed in surprise.

Suddenly, something substantial gripped her arm to replace the tingling of Sam's touch. She was kept from going under, pulled away from the warmth into cold hard reality.

"I got you. Don't worry, Vivien. I got you," a man said.

Why did the voice sound like she was in trouble? She was fine.

Vivien didn't have the energy to fight as her legs dangled before her. She was towed through the water. When her feet finally touched the ground, she stumbled on the uneven terrain. Soon she was falling. Her back hit the firm, wet sand. Freezing waves lapped her legs.

Vivien blinked in surprise as Troy crawled on the ground next to her. His hair and clothes were wet. He breathed hard as if he'd run across the sand to get to her. He leaned over her, his head blocking out the night sky as he looked into her eyes.

"Good, you're breathing." He nodded and stared at her chest as if to confirm his own statement.

Vivien tried to speak, but she was too weak to answer. Her eyes didn't want to stay focused.

"You're shivering. We have to get you inside. Can you walk?" he asked, not giving her time to answer as he lifted her into his arms. He cradled her against his chest as he carried her away from the water, away from Sam.

"No, wait," Vivien demanded, trying to grasp to any sliver of sanity she had. She struggled against his hold and pushed at his chest, forcing him to drop her feet.

Vivien hurried as fast as she could back toward the waterline, searching for her phone in the sand. When she found it, the device was dripping wet. She shook it a few times and tried to make it turn on so she could use the camera.

"Vivien, you need to get inside where it's warm," Troy insisted.

"Wait, no. I have to see..." She shook the phone harder, willing it to get dry enough to work. It didn't. "Do you have a phone?"

"Not on me. It's at the house." Troy pulled her by her elbow, forcing her to walk with him. She fought for a few feet before finally giving in. The breeze caused her clothes to sting as they slapped against her flesh. Her teeth chattered.

Troy looked like he wanted to say something but held his tongue. It only was when they'd made it onto dry sand that she realized she no longer wore her shoes. The numbing sensation that had made the ocean feel so warm and inviting started to drain from her body.

She must have looked like a complete lunatic

trying to walk into the ocean in the middle of the night.

"Nice night for a swim," she said through her chattering teeth, trying to make a joke.

"Seriously? What the hell were you thinking?" he demanded under his breath. He slipped his arm behind her back to continue to force her to walk alongside him. "Were you trying to kill yourself?"

"Why would I want to kill myself?" Vivien countered in surprise at the question. Of course that's not what she was doing. "I love me."

"Are you drunk?" he persisted.

"Not that I know of," she said, even though she felt a little dizzy. "Why? You offering to buy me a drink?"

His frown deepened. "This isn't funny. You could have died."

"I know how to swim. I don't think I was in that much danger."

"Do you know how dangerous the water can be at night?" He suddenly stopped and looked around. "Where's that roommate of yours? Is she out here too? You should know better than to be out in the water at night."

Even though she was freezing and wanted nothing more than to get inside out of the breeze.

Vivien rotated away from him to roll out of his hold. Her eyes narrowed. "Did you just chastise me? I'm sorry. Do I look like some teenager you caught out after curfew? I'm a grown-ass woman, and you can kiss my ass if you think you have any right to lecture me about what I do."

The argument might have been more convincing if her teeth weren't still trying to chatter, and if a strand of her hair hadn't plastered itself to her chin. She swiped at it a few times before managing to unstick it from her face.

"Well, I—" he began.

"If I want to swim naked in the middle of winter, that's on me. I appreciate you coming in to get me because you were worried, but I don't need the lecture."

"You're drunk," he concluded. "I will assume your meeting today had something to do with this?"

"I haven't had a drop," she insisted.

"You're slurring your words," he said, his tone completely calm and rational, "and your friends already mentioned you were drinking margaritas tonight."

Vivien lost her train of thought at the slow drawl of his words. She did feel a little like she was drunk, but that wasn't possible. "I'm not..."

His lip twitched to the side as if he weren't taking her seriously, and he couldn't quite decide if he wanted to yell at her some more or laugh at her.

"Why are you looking at me like that?" she asked.

"I'm fine if you want to keep berating me for rescuing you, but maybe we should do it inside?" He gestured toward the houses. "I'm freezing, and you're turning blue."

"I *am* cold," she admitted, trying to rub her arms with chilly hands. She still held her phone, but the device hadn't turned on. The haze from her mind was beginning to clear the farther she walked away from the water. "Maybe I can berate you later?"

"It's a date." Troy slipped his hand behind the small of her back. He was gentler than before as he guided her up the slight incline to the path.

"What were you doing out here?" she asked.

"Walking the shoreline. It's peaceful, and I sometimes have trouble sleeping," he said. "The fresh air helps me clear my mind."

They passed between the trees. Her back gate had been left open. She fingered her phone, wondering if the spirit had returned and was walking through the fence even now.

The light to her bedroom had been turned on. Heather was awake.

"Come on. Let's get you warmed up." Even though Troy was undoubtedly cold from the water, he seemed more concerned with her well-being than his own. He tried to lead her toward his house.

Vivien started to follow him without thinking, but a light came on near the side door of her kitchen. She heard footsteps coming down the stairs toward the backyard.

"Viv?" William's voice called. "Are you out here?"

"I didn't realize you had more company," Troy said. "Is that your boyfriend?"

The question was obviously him fishing about her personal life, but she answered truthfully anyway.

"That's William Warrick. He's like my brother. He is, in fact, the brother to my friend Heather," Vivien said. "He's dating my roommate."

"Oh." Troy smiled. "So not your boyfriend."

"Are you flirting with me? Now?" She shivered.

"I've been trying to flirt with you since we met. Nice of you to finally notice." Troy nodded toward his house. "Want to come over and get warmed up?"

"I should go home." It was right there, after all. "My friends are looking for me."

"Viv?" William appeared in the backyard.

"I'm here," Vivien answered. She started to walk toward William, only to stop. "Hey, thanks for pulling me out of..."

Troy had disappeared. She looked into the shadows between their houses, not seeing him.

"...the water," she finished weakly.

CHAPTER SIX

"Viv, who are you talking to?" William asked as he rushed across the lawn toward her. He wore pajama bottoms and a t-shirt. It was clear he was there to spend the night with Lorna.

"The neighbor," Vivien said. "What are you doing out here?"

"Heather woke up and discovered that you were gone. You're not answering your phone. She's worried about you," William answered. He lifted a hand to touch her shoulder, only to pull back in surprise to find it wet. "What in the world, Vivien? What happened? You're soaked."

William instantly pulled off his t-shirt and wrapped it around her shoulders. The body heat from the material helped fight the chill. He walked her toward the kitchen door.

The light struck them as they went up the stairs. She gave a small laugh. Furry creatures covered his pants. "Are you wearing teddy bear pajamas?"

"Grizzly bears," he corrected as he reached for the door to pull it open. "They're manly."

"If you say so." Vivien gave a weak cough.

He yelled, "Found her!"

"Vivien?" Heather and Lorna called out in unison. They appeared in the doorway from the hall at the same time.

"We've been calling you," Heather said. "Why didn't you answer your phone?"

Lorna had a jacket pulled onto one arm. "We were just about to come to look for you."

"Phone's dead." Vivien put her cell phone on the counter.

"Are you...?" Heather rushed toward her. "What happened?"

"I saw Sam," Vivien said. "He led me to the ocean."

"Why would he lead you into the ocean?" Lorna touched Vivien's head. "William, go start a warm shower. She's freezing. We need to get her temperature up."

William instantly went to do as his girlfriend bid.

"Good call," Heather said. "Come on, Viv. We need to get you warmed up."

"I saw Sam with my phone." Vivien wanted to tell them everything but was finding it difficult to get a coherent story out.

"Why did Sam take your phone?" Lorna asked.

"No. I saw him on my phone," Vivien said. "Sam led me to the ocean, and Troy pulled me out."

"Troy was with you?" Lorna shared a look with Heather.

Her friends wedged themselves under each of her arms and dragged more than walked her toward her bedroom. She felt their worry for her. The concern overwhelmed her own confused emotions.

"Does she feel quiet to you?" Heather asked. "I mean her feelings. Do they feel quiet?"

"Yes." Lorna nodded, and they walked her faster. "Something's not right about this."

"Sam wanted to go swimming," Vivien said, "but I thought the bonfire would be more like the old days."

"Viv, hon, I love you, but you're not making any sense right now," Heather said.

William came into the hall. "Shower's on."

"Thanks, babe," Lorna said.

"You might as well go to bed," Heather told him. "Unless you want to see Viv naked."

"Call if you need me," William answered, quickly leaving them alone.

Heather pulled at Vivien's sweater as they walked her toward the bathroom. She tossed it into the sink. The sound of the shower caught her attention.

"He touched me," she tried to explain, needing them to know but unable to find the right way to say the words. It was as if her thoughts were held hostage where only moments of clarity could surface.

Heather and Lorna pushed her into the shower with her clothes on. The warmth hit her skin, and she gave a violent shiver as it chased away the cold.

"There you are," Heather said. "I feel you coming back to us. Lift your hands. Give me the t-shirt."

"Do you got this? I can go make her tea," Lorna said. "It might help with the agitation."

"Chamomile," Heather said by way of agreement.

Lorna nodded. "Scream if you need help. I'm just going to start the kettle."

"Heather," Vivien grabbed her hand to stop her from lifting her shirt. "He touched me."

"Who? The hottie neighbor?" Heather asked.

"Sam touched me. He was trying to show me something in the water."

"You know for a fact that it was Sam you were with?" Heather jerked the shirt up, forcing Vivien to lift her arms. "We thought the demon was Glenn, so I'm going to have to hear you say you actually saw Sam's face."

"I saw him glow." Vivien closed her eyes as the warm soaked deeper into her body, and she stopped shivering. She felt Heather systematically stripping her down to her underwear but didn't care. "I wanted him to come back to me, and he has."

"Shower first. Then you can tell me all about it." Heather grabbed a loofah and squirted soap on it. The water cascaded over her clothes and hair, but she didn't appear worried about herself. She leaned over and began washing the sand off Vivien's calves and feet.

"You don't have to do that. You're getting all wet," Vivien protested.

"Shut up and lift your foot. You're lucky I love you, or else I'd be screaming at you right now about going out in the ocean by yourself. That was very stupid, Viv. You know what the currents are like. You could have died and we wouldn't have known to even look for you there."

"I know. I love you, too." Vivien smiled, braced her arm, and weakly lifted a foot. "You're pretty good at this."

"Well, you know, when I'm not remodeling houses, running theaters, summoning demons, or fighting crime, I moonlight as a foot washer. It's a passion of mine."

Vivien laughed. "When did you fight crime?"

"That youngest Larsen kid was skateboarding on the sidewalk downtown. I stopped him," Heather said.

"My hero," Vivien drawled with another laugh, lifting her other foot. "But I didn't think that was illegal."

"It's not, but his kickflip without pads and a helmet should be. That kid has no balance. I've seen him trip over his own feet walking."

"Wait, are you talking about Tommy Larsen? Oh, yeah, that kid should not be on wheels. Every time I talk to his mother in passing, I get the impression of minor emergency hospital visits. The first couple of times I thought it was a warning that I needed to do something, that someone was hurting her. But talking to Melissa at the ER, it turns out Mrs. Larsen has a boys-will-be-boys mentality when it comes to raising her five sons."

Heather's gaze dropped as she finished washing Vivien's leg. Vivien felt a wave of sorrow climb up her body before Heather pulled her hand away. She was thinking of her own son.

Vivien reached for Heather's head, touching it lightly. "I'm sorry. He was a great kid, and you were the best mom. I miss him too."

Heather nodded. "Thank you."

The water hit Heather's face, but Vivien knew tears slid down her friend's cheeks. Julia had said they were supposed to help each other heal. She wasn't sure what Julia thought they could do to help ease Heather's brand of pain, but whatever it was, Vivien would do it.

"It hits me at the oddest times like a sledgehammer." Heather stood, stepped out of the shower, and grabbed a towel off the rack. She held it for Vivien.

"Use it. I'll grab a robe," Vivien said, nodding toward Heather's wet clothes. "Borrow whatever you want. Comfy clothes are in the bottom drawers."

Heather blotted herself with the towel. Vivien turned off the shower and stepped out. It had warmed her, but she still felt weak. She cleared her throat a few times. It felt scratchy and sore.

"I have tea," Lorna announced.

"Turn around if you don't want an eyeful of my lady parts," Vivien warned, pushing her wet panties from her hips and wiggling out of her bra. Heather averted her attention as she left the bathroom. Vivien grabbed the terrycloth robe from a hook and slipped it over her body.

Lorna set the mug on a coaster on the nightstand. "Your color is looking better."

Vivien made her way to the bed, not bothering to take off the robe. She crawled under the covers. Heather took a change of clothes to the bathroom and shut the door.

"What happened tonight?" Lorna asked.

"I heard the motion sensor go off. It woke me up. I thought it was William coming over." She looked at her nightstand. The phone charger was still there, but her dead phone was in the kitchen. "But it was Sam. I know it."

"I don't see anyone here with us now." Heather came from the bathroom.

"I think we all should try to sleep," Vivien said. "I don't know about you, but I'm exhausted."

Lorna nodded and started walking toward the bedroom door. She waited as Heather crawled into bed next to Vivien. She let her hand hover near the light switch. "No more adventures tonight."

"Yes, Mom," Vivien answered with a small smile as she leaned up to take a sip of tea. When she lay back down, Lorna turned off the lights and shut the door.

"You have to be more careful, Viv," Heather whispered. "I don't know why Sam would lead you into danger, but I can't lose you. I need you to be smarter."

Vivien sighed and nodded even though it was dark and Heather couldn't see her. "I will. I promise."

CHAPTER SEVEN

Morning brought with it a clarity she hadn't had the night before. Correction, the *late* morning brought with it a clarity Vivien hadn't had the night before. Walking into the ocean after a spirit—even if that spirit were Sam—had been incredibly stupid. She knew the dangers of the ocean current and cold temperatures.

After the late-night adventure, they'd all ended up sleeping in. Well, everyone except William. He got up early enough to leave, buy donuts, banana nut muffins, and lattes, and then return before the rest of them awoke.

"You are a keeper," Lorna murmured against William's mouth as he leaned in for a kiss. She held a latte in one hand and a donut in the other. As a couple, they were adorable.

"Deal. You have to keep him," Heather said, teasingly giving her brother away. "No take backs. He's yours. Pleather couches and all."

"Why do you always have to make fun of my couches?" William protested. "They're cool."

"Because they have cup holders built in," Vivien answered.

"So? Your decor looks like it's from the nineties," William countered. He worked as a contractor, building houses in a new development. Despite the fact he hung framed football jerseys on his wall, he wasn't at a complete loss when it came to an understanding of interior design.

"Shows what you know," Vivien countered. "Early two-thousands."

"I stand corrected." William chuckled. "But it doesn't make it cool."

"I get your point. It's high time I redecorated. I'm thinking reclaimed wood, farmhouse style," Vivien said, glancing around as if the space would give her some indication what she should do with it, "or maybe shabby chic? Beach cottage might be too obvious, but then again, it could be fabulous. What do you think, roomie?"

"I think this is your house and you should design it however makes you happy," Lorna answered.

"So posters of half-naked guys and bar darts?" William inquired. "Maybe some neon signs?"

"I do like where your head is at," Vivien joked with a serious nod. "And maybe a full-size replica of Michelangelo's 'David' for the front lawn."

"Classy," Heather drawled, pulling the lid from her latte and setting it on the counter. "I'm sure your friend Troy will enjoy walking out to a naked statue every morning."

"Sure he will. He's an academic, and Michelangelo is popular with that crowd." Vivien grinned as she pulled a glazed donut from the box. "The naked guy is serious art."

"Classy and classical," Heather amended.

"Does anyone else feel like they have a hangover this morning?" Vivien suppressed a yawn. Her mind and body felt sluggish.

"No," Lorna set down her latte and reached the back of her hand to touch Vivien's forehead to test her temperature. "Do you feel sick from being in the water last night?"

The tingling of the touch didn't surprise Vivien, but as her thoughts began to clear, she realized Lorna was trying to take some of the fatigue for herself. She slapped Lorna's hand away. "Stop that."

Lorna swayed on her feet and touched her head. "I see what you mean. Did you take anything last night? Sleeping pills? This reminds me of being pill drunk."

"Pill drunk?" William inquired.

"When you take cold medicine or painkillers or whatever and you feel—" Lorna shrugged. "—kind of drunk. Woozy."

"High," Heather clarified.

"I've never heard that phrase before," he said.

"That's because you're a boring fuddy-duddy," Vivien teased.

"Not everyone can be a party animal like you, Viv," William answered. "What were you thinking last night when you went swimming with Troy?"

"I wasn't swimming *with* Troy." Vivien frowned, studying her donut as she pinched off a small piece and brought it to her mouth.

"Making out by the shore, then?" William scrunched up his face. "All I know is you looked flushed, wet, and were mumbling some strange excuses when we caught you."

"You didn't catch me, you found me." Instead of eating, Vivien threw the piece of food at his head.

William snapped his mouth to catch it and then grinned with victory as he chewed in exaggeration.

"Troy just happened to be walking by, and he pulled me out of the water. I was..." She didn't want to tell him. "I was following Sam."

"I take it this has something to do with the séance you ladies were planning last night?" William's tone revealed that he still wasn't too pleased with the idea of them dabbling in magic. He looked at Lorna. "I thought you said everything was fine?"

"It was," Lorna answered guiltily. "No reason to think there are demons."

It wasn't any secret that until a few weeks ago, when William had been knocked unconscious by the same demon that had gone after Lorna, he'd spent his entire life denying the existence of the supernatural. He'd been raised by a mother who'd hated the Warrick family legacy she'd married into, and by nature, William usually came at things from a logical perspective.

Vivien was impressed by how far he'd come. He now at least admitted ghosts were real, even if he didn't share the same enthusiasm for talking to the dead that the three friends had. And he no longer flinched and felt compelled to denounce Julia as a con artist every time someone mentioned his grandmother. That in itself was genuine progress.

When no one readily answered, he added, "It's okay. You can talk about it in front of me. What happened last night?"

Heather gave Vivien a pointed look.

"Lorna didn't lie. We have no reason to believe that a demon crossed over into our world," Vivien said.

"But?" William insisted.

"It didn't go very well. We did everything right, but..." Vivien struggled to put her feelings into words. This was definitely a new problem for her. Typically her psychic senses made her sure of herself. Half the time she couldn't shut up. Now she felt like she was fumbling around for what to say.

"Sam didn't leave like Glenn did," Lorna said. "He passed through the circle and broke the vases in the front room."

"I felt him inside me," Vivien added. She studied the half-eaten donut, suddenly not hungry. "I smelled him. I had forgotten how he always smelled like the beach. But there was so much pain there too. Even now I can feel the ache, the burning. I think he needs our help. I don't think he's in a," her voice caught, "in a good place."

"Burning? Was he on fire when you saw him last night?" William asked, confused. "Is that why you went to the ocean? To put out the flames?"

"No, later last night he wasn't burning, he was," Vivien gestured helplessly, *"friendly?"*

"A friendly ghost?" William seemed even more skeptical. He looked at Lorna. "I thought you said you weren't drinking last night."

"We weren't," Lorna said. She rubbed William's arm. "Let her tell it."

Vivien took a deep breath and then attempted to tell them everything that had happened after she woke up to the motion alarm. The story was stunted and inarticulate, but she managed. There was no point in hiding anything. When she'd finished, William was frowning, Heather gave her a sad smile, and Lorna nodded her head.

"So, you didn't see his face," Heather concluded. "Just light. You can't say for sure that it was Sam."

"Who else could it have been?" Vivien asked. "Does it make sense that we called Sam, but another ghost just suddenly showed up and wanted to take me for a romantic stroll by the water?"

"*Into* the water," William muttered.

Vivien ignored William's comment. "We all saw

Sam in the living room, so we know he's here. It had to be him leading me to the water."

"We called Glenn and got Glenn and a demon," Lorna said.

"This ghost didn't attack me," Vivien insisted. "I didn't feel scared."

"But he did try to lure you to your death," William reasoned. "What if it's another kind of demon? Lorna and I went up against a devil dog-man. Maybe this one is more like a pied piper."

"I never said he tried to lure me to my death. I said he led me to the water." Vivien frowned.

Sam had urged her to go into the water, even forced her to walk into the depths. She remembered feeling like he wanted her to see something. As a psychic, she had to trust her feelings and instincts on this. It wasn't what it looked like from the outside. Sam wasn't trying to kill her. He'd tried to communicate with her. She was sure of it.

"I think I would know if someone meant me harm." Vivien had squished the glazed donut into a flat, uneven ring. She set it on the countertop. "I mean, this is me we're talking about. If there is one thing I know, it's to trust my instincts when it comes to people."

Heather pressed her lips tightly together and stared at the floor.

"Like now. I know you want to say something, so just say it." Vivien gestured at Heather, urging her to speak.

"We need to talk to Julia," Heather said.

"That is not what you wanted to say," Vivien said in exasperation. Sure, now her gift decided to give her perfect clarity into what her friends were thinking. Where was that clarity when she was following a spirit, or when she was talking to Troy? "You want to tell me that my reading ghosts might not be the same as my reading humans. You want to tell me I'm naïve if I don't believe that walking into the ocean in the middle of the night is ill-conceived at best, and at worst, the ghost was trying to kill me."

"Well..." Heather gave a small nod.

"You don't think I know that?" Vivien exclaimed. "You think I don't know I sound like a crazy person? I know there is a chance it's not Sam, but what if it is? What if he is trying to tell me something? What if he—?"

She shut her mouth.

"What if he what?" Lorna prompted.

Vivien shook her head. "Nothing. I don't know what I was going to say."

133

Lorna and Heather reached forward at the same time, each woman grabbing one of Vivien's arms. They held tight as the transfer of emotions began to flow. Vivien felt a shiver as the static charge lifted her hair. She felt Heather and Lorna's concern for her. No, it was more than that. They were concerned *about* her.

Lorna gave a small gasp and whispered, "Oh, no."

Heather was a little more vocal. "Dammit, Viv."

"What?" William reached for his sister's shoulder. A loud *snap* sounded as the contact shocked him. He jerked his hand back in surprise. "Whoa."

Lorna let go of Vivien. "William?"

"I felt..." He looked around at the women and waved his hands to encompass them. "You all have a lot of feelings going on in there."

"It's intensified because we're touching and—" Lorna began.

"Like you're not full of feelings?" Heather interrupted. "You think I want to sense what you think about Lorna?" She gave a small shiver. "I need brain bleach and a lobotomy."

"Vivien?" Lorna asked, keeping them on topic. "Did you think you could bring Sam back from the dead?"

"You séanced Glenn," Vivien said.

"We *séanced* Glenn." Heather didn't take her eyes from her. "We didn't bring him back for good."

"Wait, you're trying to make a Sam zombie?" William inquired. "No offense, but won't that be gross? Why? Have you thought this through?"

"Ew, no." Vivien curled her lip in disgust.

"Viv, tell me bringing him back from the dead wasn't our intent when we were doing the séance," Heather stated.

Vivien bit her lip.

"Vivien!" Heather insisted.

"I can't tell you that. I mean, yeah, maybe that was my intent. I miss him so much, and you said it yourself, Julia told you that we were meant to use our new magic to help each other get over our pain. So why can't that mean we get to bring Sam back? Can you imagine if it works? If we can do that?" Vivien stopped short of mentioning Heather's son, but she could see her friend was thinking of the possibility.

"I think we need to summon Julia," Lorna said. "We're basing a lot of our decisions on what she said about helping each other. If you think about it, that's a vague directive."

"I'm not sure you should use grandma as your

guru," William said. "She was pretty out there in life. I don't think that would have changed much."

"If you intended for Sam to come back from the dead, that would explain how the séance went wrong, why he broke free from the circle," Heather said.

Vivien knew her friends were frustrated with her. Heather had been adamant about focusing their intentions, and Vivien had used their combined power to try to do more. "I'm sorry. There should have been no risk to any of us. Sam was all about love. I didn't think it would go badly."

Her heart belonged to Sam. It always had. She closed her eyes briefly, seeing his chapped lips move. She'd tried to keep moisture on them, but nothing had seemed strong enough to help.

"There is only us. I'll be watching you. Save your heart for me. It's mine."

"I will be there this time when you talk to Julia." William moved closer to Lorna and slipped an arm around her waist as if unconsciously trying to protect her from the unknown.

"I don't think—" Heather began to deny her brother's request.

"She's my grandmother too," William interrupted.

Heather looked at Lorna and then Vivien.

"I don't see why he can't be there," Vivien said.

"Damn straight I can be there. I need to protect my girls." William pulled Lorna closer to his chest and tried to look stern.

Vivien arched a brow. "I changed my mind. I know you did not just say that."

William's mouth twitched a little to show he'd been teasing to lighten the mood. "Protect my women?"

"Somehow that sounds so much worse." Vivien gave a slight laugh. "Speaking of protectors, I should probably thank Troy for fishing me out of the water. The man undoubtedly thinks I'm a lunatic."

"You're lucky he was there," Heather said.

"Maybe you should take him a muffin and thank him," Lorna suggested. "It's the neighborly thing to do."

"All right." Vivien automatically reached for a muffin. She stopped mid-action and frowned. "Why do I feel like you're both scheming?"

"We can tell you like him," Lorna said. "You just need a small push."

"Yes, I do like him. He's attractive and smart. He's a nice guy," Vivien said, with a shake of her head, "but he's not Sam. I don't see any reason to lead him on when I can't be serious about him. It would be mean to pursue him."

Especially when she couldn't rid herself of the hope that she could magically bring Sam back to her, somehow, someway.

"Honey, listen to me." Heather grabbed Vivien's hand and held it tight so she couldn't pull away. She felt her friend's emotions coming at her through the connection as if trying to convince her of Heather's sincerity. "Sam is gone. I wish he weren't, but he is. The dead don't come back to life. Not in any way that's permanent. Not in any way that you need. And definitely not in any way that you want."

All of Heather's concerns rushed into her. Desperation tinged all of the emotions.

"You don't have to be so worried about me," Vivien said, trying to pull her hand away.

Heather refused to let go. "You were young when you were with him. I don't think you've considered what that means for you now. You've grown so much. He hasn't."

"Are you saying I'm too old?" Vivien demanded.

"Be mad at me if you want, but you know better than that." Heather dismissed the question. "If a young man were going to stimulate you and give you what you need intellectually, you would have kept one of them around longer than a night. I'm not judging. I'm glad you have fun. But, at this point, can you say you want a twenty-something hanging on your couch playing video games all day? You are not that person anymore."

"Wait, I don't—" Vivien began, not liking where this lecture was heading. She hated that her friend had valid points.

"Can you say with certainty that this is what Sam would want?" Heather didn't let up. "It's been so long, maybe where he's at is a better place."

Vivien couldn't accept that Sam wouldn't want to live if given a chance. He'd been so full of life.

"No one is saying you can't still love him, but you are allowed to love more than one person in your life. You can have two great loves. You can have three, or four, or a dozen. And in doing so, you're not betraying those who came before. Love isn't like that. You don't get a finite amount of it."

"Heather, you're hurting me." Vivien again tried to pull her hand away.

"Good. Then maybe you'll hear me this time. I've told you before that Sam would want you to be happy. He wouldn't want this. He wouldn't want you drowning yourself in the ocean trying to find him." Still she held on tight. A tear slid down her cheek.

"And so help me, Viv, I need you to feel this. I can't lose anyone else I love. I don't have the capacity to survive more heartache. It would break me. I'm barely holding on by a thread as it is some days. So call it selfish. Call me codependent or needy. I don't care."

A dam broke loose inside of Heather, flooding Vivien with emotion, even more than before. She gasped at the onslaught.

"I love you, Viv. You're like a sister to me." Heather finally released her hand and swiped at her tears. "But so help me, I sometimes want to throttle you until you stop being stupid."

"Heather, I..." Vivien looked at her hand and stretched her fingers. The flood of emotions had stopped, but the aftermath remained. What could she say? In those few moments, Heather had dropped part of the wall around her heart. She let Vivien peek into the depths of her pain, not just the hard shell she kept around it.

"Just..." Heather sighed. "Be smarter."

Vivien nodded.

Lorna gave Heather a sad smile and lightly patted her shoulder.

William put his arm around his sister and pulled

her against his side in a hug. "We will not let anything happen to her."

"And you," Heather said, nudging him in the gut with her elbow. She looked at Lorna. "Or you. Like it or not, you're part of this family now too. There's no getting rid of us."

"Like I'd want to." Lorna tried to smile, but it didn't reach her eyes. Heather's mini-breakdown had affected her as well.

"Okay." Vivien nodded. "I hear you, Heather. I promise all of you that I'll be more careful."

CHAPTER EIGHT

VIVIEN KNEW her friends wanted her to thank Troy for his middle-of-the-night rescue, and if things had been different, she probably would have. If someone did something nice for you, you said thank you. That was just good manners. But something stopped her.

The idea of going over there made her feel like she was betraying Sam. Not just his memory, but Sam himself. It was different when he existed on a separate plane, but now he was here. Logically, she knew Sam wouldn't be mad about her talking to another man. He had never been possessive or jealous. The betrayal came with how she felt when she was with Troy.

Feelings didn't have to make sense. She'd

divorced Rex. It had been a conscious decision, a severing. So, of course, she couldn't cheat on Rex.

But Sam had died. Her feelings for him didn't end. If anything, she'd carried them like a torch for the last twenty years. Had things been different, they would still be married. So, if he were undead, did that mean that they picked up where they left off? The vows said *til death do us part*, but there wasn't guidance for *til undeath do us rejoin*.

She'd seen Sam's face during the séance. If he were here, how could she show interest in another guy? That didn't seem right.

What was that clever saying? What separated humans from beasts was that they weren't slaves to their impulses? People had the choice to act or not? People weren't animals?

She couldn't remember the exact words, but the sentiment was there.

Vivien had never cheated in her life, and she would not break that streak now. If Sam were back, she owed it to both of them to focus on those feelings.

Plus, there was the fact her claircognizant gifts weren't working all that well. She touched the ring on her forefinger, feeling the smooth stone. Things she should know where cloudy when she was around

Troy. Her brain hyper-focused on everything around her, and she kept missing what was right in front of her. Troy confused things at a time when she needed to be clearheaded.

However, that didn't explain last night. No one else had been around, and she'd still been fuzzy after Troy pulled her out of the water. Blaming him wasn't fair. It might not be his influence at all.

Vivien hated this confusion. Her gifts hadn't been this erratic since she was younger, and never this powerful. She felt like a hormonal teenager with her thought and feelings all over the place. She was one angsty, impulsive decision away from doing something she'd regret.

Her mind mocked as the overly placid sound of her childhood sex education teacher filled her thoughts. *"Your body is changing. New and wondrous things are happening inside you. It's natural to notice boys, but you must never act on those impulses until after marriage. Vivien, are you paying attention?"*

Mrs. Roberts preached abstinence, but that was not what she practiced every Thursday afternoon in the football coach's office.

Vivien tried to focus her wayward thoughts as she glanced out of the passenger side window. She held her new cell phone, absently bouncing the device with her fingers. Lorna and William sat in the back seat. After taking her by the cellular store for the replacement, Heather drove the four of them to the theater to talk to Julia.

Vivien saw an adolescent girl on her bicycle and knew she had a crush on an older boy. The woman in the front yard of a house secretly hated daisies because her husband had dated a woman named Daisy in college. The man on a riding lawn mower purposefully cut his grass too long so he'd have an excuse to mow again sooner. He also crooned show tunes in his underwear when his wife wasn't home.

All this useless information found its way into her brain like a personal reality TV show. Before they'd put on the rings, Vivien would have been able to see Troy's intent to ask her. That trick was easy. It was also how she knew which guys in a bar would be up for some fun, and not possessive. Before Troy tried to ask her, she would have artfully dodged the question and moved him firmly in the friend zone. The thoughts of more would never have been considered a possibility—by either of them.

"Vivien? You okay?" Lorna asked, leaning forward between the seats.

"I'm getting a little bit of a headache from all the

impressions I'm picking up. Also, no one eat at that fancy Italian restaurant. We just passed one of the cooks and, well, just don't."

"All right then. So, pizza date instead?" William asked Lorna.

"Yeah. Maybe that would be best," Lorna agreed, as they instantly took Vivien's word for it.

"And I've been thinking about what you were saying," Vivien continued. "I know Troy is a nice guy, and I am attracted to him, but it's not going to work. I can't trust my instincts right now, and I'm pretty sure he thinks I'm an idiot. I said all kinds of stupid things when I gave him a ride home, and then he had to fish me out of the water. Trust me, no guy in their right mind would still want to ask me out after that. So I think we should just mark that off as not happening."

"So what I hear you saying is, you're hoping that lame excuse will convince us not to pressure you to see him again," William said. "As my buddy Will wrote, 'The lady doth protest too much, methinks.'"

"I didn't know you were friends with Shake-speare," Lorna joked.

"I'm a man of mystery," William answered.

Vivien turned around in her seat and arched a

MICHELLE M. PILLOW

brow to get William to shut up. It didn't work. He kept talking.

"I mean, speaking from a completely male perspective here, we're not so easily turned off when it comes to someone we like," William continued. "You will have to try harder than saying something stupid."

"Wait. Are you saying I say stupid things and you still like me?" Lorna asked.

"That's what I heard," Vivien said, eager to turn the conversation away from her.

"Of course not. You are the most beautiful, brilliant, sweet, giving, smart, lovely person I have ever met," William said.

"Nice save," Heather said.

"My point is, if Troy likes you, your late-night swim probably activated his male-driven hero complex. Face it, you're his damsel in distress now, and he's your knight in shining armor." William smirked, his tone light. "It's all marriage and babies from here."

"Heather, I'm going to need you to pull over so I can beat up your brother," Vivien said, keeping her eyes forward. Under her breath, she muttered, "Damsel in distress who needs saving, my ass."

"I didn't make the rules," William continued to tease. "It's biological."

"Didn't you flunk biology?" Heather asked.

"No. I got a C-minus," William answered. "I stand by my point."

"If you don't want to date Troy, we won't press the issue," Lorna said. "We'll support you whatever you decide."

Vivien smiled. Lorna had a natural sweetness about her.

Heather turned onto Main Street. The historic brick buildings were a point of pride in Freewild Cove, but there was one building that stood out amongst the rest—Warrick Theater. Compared to similar theaters in small towns, it wasn't anything special. It only had a little over a hundred seats in the auditorium. Heather often held screenings of movies from the 1980s and '90s, and there was a stage for live performances.

Julia Warrick commissioned it over a hundred years ago. The interior needed a coat of paint, but Vivien didn't dare say that to Heather. It had the same gold and burgundy sponge-painted walls that had been there when Heather inherited the property from her grandmother. With the building's historical status, it took special permission from the city to make any changes, which was another way of saying it would take an act of God, and even then the council would still debate for three years.

What made the theater stand out was that it was commissioned by a woman, and not just any woman —a renowned medium and spiritualist. Julia held séances, and people came from across the country to see her perform. But Julia was much more than that —she'd been a bootlegger, a pot grower, owned a hotel, and even had a small stint as a burlesque dancer.

The woman was a freaking legend and Vivien's personal hero.

Heather found parking close to the entrance. She led the way to the smaller door next to a long row of glass security doors and unlocked it to let everyone inside. They entered the front lobby. To the left were restrooms, the theater office, storage, and a door that led up to Lorna's former apartment. To the right was a hallway with access to the side alley. The concession stand had been stocked and cleaned. Vivien knew that it was Heather's doing. Lorna had not been back to the theater since the last demon attack.

Lorna walked across the lobby to stare at the floor where Heather and William had found her after the demon had attacked the first time. She then turned in a slow circle looking around. "The air feels lighter in here. I think the smudging helped. I don't feel afraid."

Vivien agreed but didn't verbalize it.

"Julia usually hangs around the seating area," Heather said, leading the way into the auditorium. William and Lorna followed her.

Vivien began to go after them but felt a shiver of apprehension and stopped. She turned to the row of glass doors. The sidewalk in front of the theater was empty. Cars drove down Main Street at a leisurely pace. Nothing appeared out of the ordinary.

She looked left then right. Nothing unexpected was in the theater with her.

A tiny, dismissive laugh almost escaped her, only to die when her eyes went back toward the glass doors. She saw someone standing across the street, staring at the theater. The glass must have been smudged because the man appeared out of focus.

No. Wait. He was not staring at the building. It felt as if he stared at *her*.

Vivien slowly walked toward the doors. Her hand lifted for the handle. The bright sunlight made it hard to see details, but her psychic senses told her she didn't imagine this.

With each step, her heart beat harder. The figure

didn't move. A car drove past, the sun reflecting off shiny metal, forcing her to blink.

The man lifted a hand and motioned, just like the spirit that had led her to the beach. Vivien felt the need to listen. She pushed the long metal security handle to open the door. A cool breeze hit her when she stepped outside, colder than it had been when she'd entered the building minutes before with her friends.

"Sam?" she whispered, knowing it had to be him. She saw the shape of him, the impression of youth and vitality. He wore shorts with no shirt.

Vivien stopped at the curb as another car went by. The reflected light caused her to blink again. She shaded her eyes. Sam raised his hand and motioned for her to join him.

She had to go. She had to see him.

How was he here? The details of his face appeared blurred as if she couldn't quite bring him into focus.

"Sam?" she asked a little louder, but not loud enough for any living person to hear her from across the street. She fought to find her voice. Every inch of her shook. Nerves bunched in her stomach and caused her to shiver.

He lifted his hand again. Vivien nodded and

stepped off the curb. She glanced to the side to make sure no cars were coming. Her heart beat heavily in her ears. In a few steps, she'd be with him.

"Sam," she managed a little louder.

The word barely left her when a horn honked loud and long. An SUV swerved past her.

"Vivien!" Heather screamed in terror.

Someone yanked her arm, roughly jerking her back. She narrowly missed being struck as a second vehicle whizzed past. William flung her into the side of Heather's car. The hard metal jarred her, and she grunted in pain. The sound of running footsteps pounded on the sidewalk as Lorna and Heather rushed toward them. Another car drove by, not as fast as the others.

"What is wrong with you?" William demanded. "Why didn't you look where you were going?"

"I..." She frowned as she looked across the street. Sam was gone. "I did. That car came out of nowhere."

"Nowhere? You looked right at it and stepped in front of traffic," Heather said. "You're lucky we were coming to get the candles out of the car."

"No, I looked. There wasn't any traffic," Vivien said. "Look both ways when crossing the street.

That's kindergarten-level stuff. Those drivers were driving like maniacs."

"No, they weren't," Lorna said.

"Is everyone all right?" a voice called.

"Yes, Melba, thank you. We're fine!" Heather shouted down the sidewalk.

"Have you seen Ace?" Melba yelled.

"No, sorry," Heather answered. "If I see your cat, I'll let you know!"

Vivien's heart beat faster as she belatedly responded to almost being hit by a car. Her legs weakened and she held onto Heather's car for support. "I didn't see it. I looked and I didn't see it. All I saw was..."

"Was what?" Lorna prompted.

"Sam. I saw Sam. He wasn't just a bright light this time. He was standing there waving at me to come over. His face was blurry, like he was a little out of focus, but I know it was him. I felt no fear. I just wanted to get to him." A tear slipped down Vivien's cheek. She had looked and the streets had been empty. He'd made her feel safe. All she could think about was getting to him. "I think I'm in serious trouble."

"Let's go inside." Heather slipped her arm

through Vivien's and held her upright. "We're starting to draw a crowd."

Vivien ignored the family that had paused a few feet away to watch them. Others had stopped across the street. The sidewalks were no longer empty.

"Heather, I was wrong," Vivien whispered as her friend led her to the unlocked door. "I made an enormous mistake. I think Sam does want to kill me."

CHAPTER NINE

THE LOVE of her life wanted her dead.

Everything inside Vivien protested that statement. Sam had not been an evil man. He'd barely been a man. They were kids playing at house, so young, so broke, so hopeful. She'd give anything to go back to that imperfect perfection.

Anything but her life.

What had she done? She'd been so desperate to get Sam back that she hadn't stopped to think about the consequences. It had never occurred to her that her desire to find a way to magically resurrect him would somehow end up with him trying to kill her and bring *her* to his afterlife.

Vivien was not ready to die. She was not one to have fatalistic tendencies. She loved being alive.

Besides, her friends needed her, and she needed them. Heather's desperation lingered inside her. It was a feeling she'd never be able to shake. And Lorna had come so far after the betrayal of her dead husband, but she still fought her doubts about her relationship with William.

Ah, William. He would never admit it, but he needed her too. He thought of her as a sister, and they bickered like siblings. William didn't let many people in, not really. He was likable and had friends, but they were buddies at best. If Lorna became hesitant about their relationship, he wouldn't know to keep pushing. He'd be respectful and back away, and it would be the biggest mistake of his life. Lorna and William belonged with each other. She'd seen it the second she witnessed the two of them walking together. They sent off a beacon any half-assed psychic could see, and Vivien was hardly half-assed.

Sometimes souls just fit. They were two pieces of the same puzzle.

Vivien's piece had been Sam. She'd felt the explosion of it when they first met, and she'd felt the unbearable agony when she lost him.

Doubts crept into her thoughts. What if too much time had passed? What if she weren't the same person? What if it wouldn't be the same? What if the only way they could be together again was with her death?

Vivien would die someday, obviously, but that would not be today. She didn't want to die to be with him, not anymore. And that bothered her.

This was the grand love of her life. This was the romance-novel love story. This was a love that defied reality and broke all the rules. Every female in her family knew these things to be true.

If those facts were accurate, then nothing else should matter. She shouldn't be thinking of Heather's feelings, or Lorna and William's relationship, or how much she enjoyed breathing and... ah fuck. Troy. She kept thinking of Troy.

She could write off Troy as a thought planted in her head by her friends. He had saved her. Maybe there was something to William's damsel-in-distress theory. Not that she was a damsel who needed a prince charming to save her, but the whole psychological hero-grateful-mistaken-love thing did happen after a daring rescue.

That didn't explain her bumbling around during the car ride. Or her attraction to him when they'd first met. Or...

"Shut up, brain," Vivien hissed under her breath.

"Viv?" Heather asked. She and Lorna were

staring at her as Vivien stood on the stage, holding one of the blue candles.

"Yeah, here," Vivien said, handing the candle toward Lorna. "I was just saying I think it's smart that we're doing this here." She gestured to the black-painted stage. "It is where Julia spent a lot of time, and I'm beginning to think maybe this is the place with the best mojo."

"That's what you were saying?" Heather asked as she placed the séance book on the floor. It was the same setup they'd used to call Glenn, and it had worked in this space.

Vivien nodded.

Heather arched a brow. "Funny, cause I distinctly heard you tell your brain to shut up."

"You know, a good friend would just let me have my lie," Vivien muttered.

"And a great friend will call you on your bull-shit," Heather countered. "If you need someone to blow sunshine up your ass, I'm sure that chick Summer is around here somewhere."

"Omigod, Summer? I haven't thought about her in years," Vivien laughed. To Lorna, she explained, "She was this super-perky cheerleader who used to tell people these strange affirmations every day—like

THIRD TIME'S A CHARM

bad internet memes before the internet was a thing. Only you can feel the sunshine of your life. Breathe and enjoy today, don't worry about tomorrow because aliens could blow us up any second. It was like she read them in some kind of calendar each morning. She was voted most likely to be sucked into a cult."

"Oh, no." Heather laughed. "That's too harsh."

"You brought her up," Vivien said. "And tell me it doesn't sound like it could be true."

"Yeah, it does, but I would have said she's the person most likely to end up writing the internet memes," Heather said.

"Well, you're nicer than me. I still haven't forgiven her for what she did to you during your junior year." Vivien watched Lorna arrange the candles on the floor around the book.

"What happened in junior year?" Lorna asked.

"Summer farted in front of a popular boy she liked and blamed it on me because I was the only other person there," Heather said. "It was foul. Teenagers are mean."

"Are you talking about the famous sauerkraut fart heard around the world?" William asked from the aisle below.

"Gee, memory lane is so much fun," Heather

drawled sarcastically. "I sure hope we can talk about this all day."

"You brought it up," Vivien said.

"Now I'm bringing it down," Heather said.

"I am so glad we're no longer teenagers," Lorna said. "I don't miss the angst at all."

"I don't miss school," Heather added. "I remember calculating how many wasted hours there were each day. In elementary school, I was convinced if we all agreed to skip lunch, recess, and time spent playing stupid games in class, we should be able to leave after three hours of actual work."

"You also wanted to skip gym," William put forth, looking up at them from in front of the stage. "I can still remember the horrified look on our mother's face as you presented your arguments to her."

"That was time wasted playing stupid games," Heather said.

"I miss the energy I had back then," Vivien said.

"You say that like you've been slowed down." Heather shook her head. "I think you're more active now than you were in high school."

"I can't see her anywhere," William said, referring to Grandma Julia. He had walked the length of the theater, studying the empty seats. "I tried feeling for her like you said, but I don't think she's here."

"She's over there," Heather automatically pointed toward her left. "I can't hear her, but she's watching us."

Vivien turned to look where Heather indicated. She wanted to see Julia like Heather did, but nothing was there.

"Anyone else hanging around?" Lorna asked.

"No. It feels like it's back to normal," Heather said.

"Yeah, normal," William whispered in disbelief under his breath, still searching the seats for a sign of his grandma. Vivien was proud of him for trying, but he was still having a hard time dealing with his belief in the supernatural.

"Okay, we're ready," Lorna said. She had lit the candles around the book.

"Where do you want me?" William asked.

"Up here with us," Heather said. "Grandma Julia always included other people in her séances. I think it will give her more energy to manifest."

William pushed his hands into the stage floor and hopped his butt onto the stage without using the stairs. He swung his legs up, stood, and then came to stand between Lorna and Heather. The four of them formed a circle around the book and then sat down.

"Just read this with us," Lorna instructed him, sharing the piece of paper Heather handed her.

Vivien glanced at the paper. It wasn't the same words they'd used to call Glenn and Sam.

"I modified it a little," Heather said. "I thought this one might work better on Julia."

The spell had been one that searched for a lost child. Vivien was surprised Heather had chosen to use it. Though, all reference to a child had been taken out.

"Join hands," Heather said. They all took hands. At the contact her hair lifted from her shoulders. She looked at William to see what effect it was having on him. He was looking upward as if he could see his shorter hair floating around his head. The lights flickered and dimmed. The candles burned brighter.

"I feel... something," William said.

"We're connected," Heather answered. "Now, shh. Concentrate on wanting to talk to Grandma Julia. I know you're nervous, but you have to push that aside."

William nodded.

The emotions from the group seemed to flow clockwise through her body, entering the side that held Lorna's hand and leaving into Heather. They became a jumbled mass as if each person shared the other's experiences. William was indeed nervous, more so than excited. Lorna was excited, but still a little nervous. Heather was worried about everyone, but not scared of her grandmother. And Vivien, well, she felt all of them more than she felt herself. It overwhelmed her, and she didn't know what she was feeling.

Heather began to read, causing everyone to join in as they said in unison, "Spirits tethered to this plane we humbly seek your guidance. Spirits search amongst your numbers for the spirit we seek. We call forth Julia Warrick from the great beyond."

Vivien watched the book, waiting for Julia to appear. When nothing happened right away, she glanced over her shoulder to the section where Heather said she saw her ancestor.

"I don't..." Vivien turned back to the book. Julia had not appeared, but the faint sound of jazz came from someplace distant. "Do you hear that?"

"No," William said.

"What?" Lorna asked.

"The clicking noise?" Heather inquired with a tilt of her head.

"No, it's like," Vivien strained to hear, "sultry..."

"Sultry?" Lorna repeated.

The music became louder as if drifting from an

invisible orchestra pit. Vivien pulled her hands from Lorna and Heather and stood. "You can't hear that? It's like a burlesque."

"Didn't Julia dance burlesque?" Lorna asked.

"Oh, hell, no, I don't want to see my grandma doing a striptease." William shut his eyes tight, only to peek through a barely opened lid.

"Not all burlesque shows were stripteases," Heather corrected.

Something took hold of Vivien's arm, lifting it to the side. She heard a sound of cheering resonate over the music. She tried to turn to her friends, but the same force took hold of her hip, causing it to rotate seductively.

"Oh, hey, what—?" Before Vivien could get out a coherent question, the room filled with light and color. The music became loud, and she saw a crowd of men in suits and ladies in gowns standing from their seats as they clapped. She looked down as something hit her thighs. It was fringe from a sparkly flapper dress. High heels lifted her ankles, so she felt like she put all her weight on her toes.

Her head jerked up, and her body began to move against her will. A smile forced its way over her mouth as she grinned. She swung her arms, kicked her legs, and shuffled her feet back and forth in time to the music. There was no way Vivien would have known this routine or half the moves her body performed, but here she was, dancing burlesque in the Warrick Theater like it was the 1920s.

A smoky female voice began to sing, but Vivien's heart pounded loudly in her ears and she barely heard the words. She felt more than saw other dancers with her. They stayed just behind her peripheral. People cheered. She tried to call out for her friends, but something had taken over her body and her consciousness was just along for the ride.

Someone grabbed her hips from behind, and she was lifted into the air, her feet kicking high over her head before she was set back down. The force of it caused her to fall forward.

Whatever it was let go of her, and she was caught by Lorna and Heather. The music and cheering stopped. Colors faded into the darkness of the theater in modern-day.

"What was that?" Heather asked. "Where did you learn to dance like that?"

Vivien breathed hard, and her heart pounded wildly. The dancing had been like a drug, a breath-taking, intoxicating feeling, and for a second, she wished the ride wasn't over. There had been freedom in the performance.

The sound of dancing feet in a music-less room caught her attention. Vivien turned to look behind her. The transparent image of Julia continued to perform the dance. But it was not Julia as she remembered her, not the grandmother in the floral-print dresses. This Julia was young and vibrant, and incredibly flexible. She swung her leg up and around with ease.

William had a sick look on his face. He covered his mouth as he watched his grandmother lean over and shake her booty for the nonexistent crowd. "Please tell me I'm not seeing this. I'm going to have to poke my eyes out later if she takes her... *omigod.*"

Julia reached behind her and unzipped her dress. She grabbed the hem and began to pull it over her head.

"Grandma!" Heather scolded before Julia could show her retro bra and panties. "Come on."

The sound of Heather's voice appeared to pull Julia from the memory. Julia disappeared, and the dress dropped to the floor before it also vanished.

"Where did she go? Is she gone?" William asked. "Is it too late to take back wanting to see her?"

"Is that what you meant when you talked about a residual haunting?" Lorna asked. "Ghost do things from the past, but they can't really control it?"

"No, she can control it, and I have never seen her do that before," Heather said. "Julia is not a residual haunting. She is very much aware of what she does."

"What if we broke her?" Lorna asked. "What if the demon did something to her soul? You said she wasn't as strong."

"That doesn't explain why Viv suddenly knew how to dance like that." Heather stayed close to Vivien, as if afraid she would start dancing again.

"It's like she was possessed," William suggested.

"That's not funny," Lorna said.

William went to his girlfriend and cupped her face. He gave her a quick, reassuring kiss.

"I don't think he's wrong," Vivien put forth. "I couldn't control my body. It felt like somebody wore me like a suit, forcing me to do those things. I had no say. It was fun, but I couldn't stop myself. I don't know how I stopped."

"Sorry that was me." The voice came from beside the book. "It's been so long since I inhabited a body, and I couldn't resist when I found one open to possession."

Vivien turned at the sound.

Julia still didn't appear the way Vivien remembered her. She was younger, more like the pictures she had seen in Heather's old trunk of family photos.

Julia wore a pantsuit with high-waisted trousers and what looked to be a smaller version of a man's shirt and suit vest. A gold chain dangled from one of her vest pockets. There was always something glamourous about how women looked in the 1920s, with finger-waved, bobbed haircuts and deep red lipstick. Even with her translucent state muting the colors, Vivien saw the details of Julia's face.

"Grandma Julia?" William slowly crept forward and lifted his hand to feel the air around the spirit.

Julia faced her grandson and lifted her hand to hover near his. She didn't touch him. "Look at you, Mr. Hard-boiled."

"Um, Heather?" William asked, leaning away as Julia moved her hand closer to him.

"Does she normally look like this?" Vivien asked.

"Sometimes." Heather gave a long sigh. "Her clothes and age change. This incarnation is a bit of a handful."

"You never said." Vivien thought Grandma looking like a 1920s bootlegger would have warranted a mention.

Heather shrugged. "No one asked."

"Seriously, Heather," William insisted, taking a slow step back as Julia kept inching closer to him. "I think there is something wrong with Grandma."

"Hard-boiled means you're a manly man," Heather said. "Don't you ever watch historical dramas?"

"No. I watch football," William stated.

"Wow, Julia, I was expecting you to look..." Vivien couldn't take her eyes away from Julia. This was a ghost. An honest-to-goodness, not-trying-to-kill-her, interactive spirit. She'd been expecting a much older woman.

"Older? Sorry, doll, my last chapter was not as fun as this one," Julia answered, her voice sounding surprisingly clear. "This is the era that defined my life. Oh, the sneaking around, the dancing, the parties, slinging hooch. William, be a good boy and butt me."

"No." William recoiled.

"Fine. I'll do it myself." Julia lifted her hand, and a lit cigarette appeared between her fingers. "That mother of yours did not raise much of a gentleman. Can't even get a lady a cigarette."

"Hi, Mrs. Warrick, I'm Lorna. I found one of your rings." Lorna lifted her hand to show the ring to the spirit. Her voice trembled a little, and Vivien knew her friend was nervous.

"I know. I led you to it," Julia answered, her tone slightly dismissing. To Heather, she said, "Took you long enough to summon me. What's a lady got to do to get attention around here? Dance a hoochie-coochie?"

"No. Definitely not," William muttered.

"I haven't been ignoring you. In fact, I have been trying to get *your* attention. You kept disappearing on me. The last thing you told me was we'd all been brought together for a reason, that we are meant to help each other heal from our individual pains." Heather moved closer to Julia, clearly not as stunned as the others when being faced with the otherworldly being. "We found the book. We found the altar. As far as I know it is still underneath the stage. I haven't been able to get back down there again to check."

"Yeah, I locked it. You don't need that old thing. It's just a prop," Julia interjected.

"We found the rings," Heather continued. "We found each other. I thought I understood what we were supposed to do with that, but now I'm not so sure."

"You have the book," Julia dismissed, taking a long drag off her cigarette. Smoke filtered from between her lips, but there was no smell as it dissipated into the air. "It's all spelled out in there. I don't think I can make it any clearer. Though the demon? What was the reason for that? Playing with those creatures is a little advanced. It was very careless of you to let it run loose in here. I would suggest you figure out the basics first."

"We didn't mean to summon a demon," Vivien said.

"Oh, then you must be much more careful, doll," Julia quipped. She waved her hand in the air, and the cigarette disappeared. The spirit slowly walked toward Lorna as if to study her face. "I'm glad you got to see that ex of yours for what he was. When I heard the whispers of your story, I knew you needed my Heather as much as she needs you and Vivien. It looks like you found peace. Have you found peace?"

"Yes." Lorna nodded. "I have, thank you."

Julia poked a transparent finger at Lorna's arm. Lorna gave a small jump of surprise at the contact, much to Julia's amusement. The spirit began to laugh, tossing back her head in her merriment.

"She's found a new boyfriend too," Vivien added. "I wouldn't be surprised if you're looking at your new granddaughter by marriage."

"You always were a bit of a gossip," Julia told Vivien with a wink. "I like it."

"Hey, at least let me ask her before you all assume," William said.

Lorna actually turned a little red at the conversation.

"Sorry." Vivien gave them a look of contrition. "Sometimes my psychic senses get the best of me."

"Can we get this conversation back on track?" Heather interrupted the banter. "Grandma, is the demon gone?"

"What a silly question." Julia arched a brow. "Is it out of the realm of existence? No, of course not. What is death for a demon? But if you want to know if it's off this plane of existence, then yes. You exorcised it."

"Okay, good." Heather nodded. "And when we called Sam, did we bring over a new kind of demon?"

"Sam didn't come. Glenn did," Julia said. "You sent him packing as well. Good riddance."

"I'm talking about last night. We were at Vivien's house, and we called Sam." Heather moved to the side to stay within Julia's eyeline when her grandmother would turn her attention to someone else.

"I wasn't invited." Julia waved a hand in dismissal. To Lorna, she said, "Glenn is where he's supposed to be."

"Where is that?" Lorna asked. Vivien felt her friend's concern. Glenn was a top-notch asshat, but he was still the father of Lorna's three children, and that bond would never completely go away.

"Oh, no, doll, nice try." Julia shook her finger at Lorna. "I'm not telling you about the afterlife. Some secrets you get after you die."

"Julia." Vivien moved to get the ghost's attention. "We need your help. I tried to bring Sam back."

"If it didn't work, try again. It's not like he's going anywhere." Julia pointed at the book. "I gave you everything you need."

"Grandma, please," Heather pleaded. "We need you to listen to what we're asking."

At the tone of her voice, Julia's form shivered and she disappeared, only to rematerialize moments later as an older version of herself. This was closer to how Vivien remembered her. Her hair had streaks of gray but was still bobbed. Her body had widened, as bodies do with age, and she wore a dark skirt with a floral blouse. She had chunky jewelry, bold like her personality.

The sassiness left Julia's tone as she said, "Why do you look so worried, love?"

"We tried to bring back Sam, Vivien's first husband, who died over twenty years ago," Heather said. "He came back, but he escaped the circle on the book and shot through Vivien's living room, breaking things."

"You should draw the circle on the floor instead. It gives more room for the spirit to move around and not build too much energy," Julia said. "The illustrations are just guides. You have to take them and make them your own. You'll know what to do. Trust your instincts. What is meant to be will come to pass."

"Julia, that's not everything. I messed up," Vivien inserted. "When Lorna and Heather intended to do the séance so I could see Sam again and find closure, I secretly wanted him to come back."

She looked at her feet and touched the ring. Her statement wasn't clear, and she knew that.

"I..." Vivien took a deep breath. "I wanted him to come back from the dead. I thought the magic you gave us might help me do that."

Saying it out loud made her feel foolish.

"I thought I could bring him back to life," Vivien clarified further. When no one spoke, she finally forced her eyes up to meet Julia's.

Julia slowly shook her head. "That's a different kind of death magic. Necromancy, zombies, soul displacements, nothing good comes from these things. And after twenty years, there would be nothing to bring back."

"I thought, I *hoped* I could bring him back as I remembered, as a living person," Vivien said. "Why not? We have these powers. We know that the impossible is possible. If we're together to heal, then that's what I need to heal."

"No. That's what you think you want," Julia said. "There is no reversal for death. It's the doorway to your next step. That fragility is what makes life beautiful. I recommend you not wish for that again."

"I think he might be trying to lure me to the other side," Vivien said. She quickly told Julia what happened in the ocean and when crossing the street. "I think he tried to kill me, and in the moment, it didn't occur to me to stop him."

"The only way for such a spell to work is for you to join him. He can't join you." Julia appeared concerned. Her hair grayed completely and wound into a bun as she stood before them, and her body became more transparent as if she were losing the energy to manifest. Her clothing shifted to a baggy housecoat and slippers.

"How do we stop it," Heather asked.

"If Sam is truly trying to kill you because of a spell you cast, then you must séance him so he comes to you, make clear to him it's over, trust yourselves, say your goodbyes, and send him on his way." Julia's voice had softened, and she shimmered slightly before disappearing.

The overhead theater lights came back on with a flicker.

"Julia?" Heather called. She looked around the theater. "I don't see her."

"That was…" William let loose a long sigh. He stood with his arm around Lorna.

"Vivien?" Lorna pushed away from William and rushed to her. She swiped her thumb over Vivien's cheek, brushing aside a tear. "We'll figure this out."

"Okay, let's do this. Let's séance Sam," William stated, clearly wanting to fix the problem immediately. "You can tell him to move on, and we can end this."

Vivien was feeling drained from the energy it took to manifest Julia, and by looking at Lorna and Heather, they were feeling it too.

"Okay," Heather said, to Vivien's surprise. She moved back toward the book to take her position for the new séance. "We'll use the same verbiage but change Julia's name to Sam."

William joined his sister. Lorna looked around the floor and picked up a couple of the papers with writing on them. She moved to sit on the floor.

Vivien was the last to join them. She wasn't

ready to say goodbye to Sam. The idea hurt too much, but she also didn't want to die so she resigned herself to reality. If there were no way to bring him back, she needed to return him where he belonged.

As she sat down on the floor, a numbness overtook her. She barely felt Heather's and Lorna's hands. The energy hummed inside her, and the lights dimmed. It all felt like it happened to someone else. All hope was gone. This was really going to be goodbye.

"I don't think I can do this," Vivien whispered to Heather, her entire body shaking.

Heather squeezed her hand tight. "You got this. You're one of the strongest women I know, Viv. This is for the best."

Vivien glanced at Lorna who nodded back to her in encouragement.

"Spirits tethered to this plane we humbly seek your guidance," Vivien felt herself saying the words with the others. "Spirits search amongst your numbers for the spirit we seek. We call forth Sam Stone from the great beyond."

The candles flickered. Their firelight projected into an image of bare feet standing on the book. She thought of Julia's advice to draw a bigger circle for the spirit to move around, but it was too late. She felt her friends' desire to help her. No it was more than a desire. It was a desperate need. They wanted to get this over with so they could save her.

The candlelight reflected inside the ghost's body, illuminating him from within. The light traveled up his naked calves to a pair of swim trunks over his bare chest and arms. She knew it was Sam before his face was revealed.

He looked at her. A smile curled his lips. Memories flooded her. The shadows of his form made it hard to see his eyes, but she didn't feel threatened by him. This did not look like a man who wanted to kill her.

He looked so young, too young to be dead.

"It's not fair that you were taken from me," Vivien said. "I've missed you so much."

He didn't speak as he stared at her, smiling.

Now that he was here, she slipped her hands out of Lorna's and Heather's. She slowly stood. Sam's eyes filled with light and became visible as his gaze lifted to follow her.

"It was selfish of me to want you to come back. I shouldn't have wished for that. I'm sure you're much happier where you are." Vivien didn't know if it were true, but she hoped it were. Her friends came to stand beside her and looked up at Sam's spirit. "I love you, Sam. I always will. Someday I'll be with you again, but not now. I can't come now. And I know that you can't come back to me, not like I want. So I'm saying goodbye. I have to move on with my life, and you have to move on with your..."

Her voice caught. She couldn't finish the sentence. Julia said she had to make him understand.

"There is only us."

"Only our hearts."

"I'll be watching you. Save your heart for me. It's mine."

Vivien had to be clear that they couldn't be together, not when she belonged with the living, and Vivien wanted to be alive.

"I'm going to date the neighbor." Vivien felt the need to explain it to him. "He's a nice guy. I deserve a nice guy. But that doesn't mean I love you any less. I will never love you any less. It's been twenty years since I lost you and I have to live my life. I can't keep..."

Her voice became choked in her throat, and she coughed.

"It's time," Heather said, taking her hand as Lorna took the other. William stood by Lorna. Heather held up a piece of paper, and they read,

"Spirit you have been found pure. We release you into the light. Go in peace and love."

Sam grinned wider and winked at her before disappearing.

"Did that do it?" William inquired, staring at where Sam had been. "Is he gone now?"

"Viv, are you okay?" Lorna asked.

Heather simply hugged her.

"If this is what closure feels like it sucks ass," Vivien muttered. She took a deep breath and tried to shake the feelings away.

Heather let go of her. "William, can you grab the book and candles for us?"

William nodded and seemed glad to have a task.

"What can we do for you?" Lorna asked.

"I need sugar and a stiff drink." Vivien watched William blow out the candles and gather them so the wax didn't spill over. "Who wants to go the Blues House Tavern with me? They have lava cake, cheese fries, and blueberry vodka with sugar rims."

"The dinner choice of champions," Heather said. "If that's what you want, then let's do it."

CHAPTER TEN

Tipsy decisions weren't always the most thought out. Vivien guessed that most people would say they led to regrets. However, in Vivien's experience, they often led to an entertaining story she told later with pride. Life was to be lived and enjoyed. Mistakes were to be learned from and sometimes laughed at. In every aspect of her existence, she had lived life to the fullest, except for one.

Love.

When it came to love, she'd bottled that feeling and locked it away with the pain of losing Sam. He became the excuse that kept her from feeling deeply for another man. He became the shield over her heart. He became the catalyst to live fully, without loving fully, without risking herself or her heart.

It wasn't closure she'd found in saying goodbye to Sam, not like she thought. There wasn't some giant weight that lifted from her heart. Her love did not lessen. However, in telling him she had to move on, she was finally able to see the possibility that maybe, just maybe, Heather was right. Perhaps a person got more than one true love in life. One feeling did not negate another.

Vivien knew walking up to Troy's front door and knocking might be a mistake, one she couldn't take back later, but still she found herself standing on his doorstep. She didn't know if Troy was some future great love, but there was no denying her attraction to him. Plus, she trusted Heather's and Lorna's assessment of the situation.

Vivien lifted her hand, only to let it drop without knocking. This wasn't a booty call type situation. Troy wasn't a one-night-stand guy. She knew that as sure as she knew her own name.

Vivien turned to go, stopped mid-step, and turned back to the house. She again lifted her hand and hesitated.

"Thank you for saving me from the water last night. Want to go make out?" she said under her breath to the door. "And I sound lame."

Vivien scrunched up her nose, dropped her

hand, and started to leave. This time she made it two steps before turning back around.

She didn't bother lifting her hand as she said to the door, "Hi, Troy. I'm not really good at this dating thing. I mean, I'm *good*. I'm really good at what you do when you're," she frowned and mumbled, "dating."

She bit her lip and scrunched up her face. Why was this so difficult? She talked to men all the time. Flirting wasn't hard. Hell, half the time all she had to do was smile.

"I like you. I know I sound like I'm all over the place when we talk. You found me walking into the ocean. And the truth is..."

The truth? She couldn't tell him she was following her dead husband into the afterlife.

"The truth is I like you." Vivien sighed and lifted her hand to knock.

"I like you too."

Vivien gasped as she spun to the side. Troy came from around the corner of the house.

"Though, I'm totally cool if you want to go with option number one and make out with me," he added with a grin.

"You heard all that." Vivien glanced toward her home.

Troy chuckled. "Yeah, I heard all that. I was going to interrupt sooner, but you looked deep in thought."

If she ran, she could be through her front door within a few seconds. How often did people need to see their neighbors anyway?

"If it helps, I'm glad I did. You aren't exactly the easiest woman to read," he said. "I thought maybe my signals were off."

"I don't think anyone has ever said that to me." Vivien laughed. "Normally they tell me I talk too much and need to keep things to myself."

"I don't know who *they* are, but I would venture to guess they aren't worth listening to." He walked around to the front step of his home. "Can I assume you'd like to come inside?"

Vivien again glanced at her house. She saw the curtain move and realized her friends were peeking at her from the window.

"Yeah, they've been watching us." Troy waved toward Lorna and Heather. The curtain dropped.

"Were you at the beach doing environmental research?" she asked, trying to make the conversation closer to normal.

"Yeah, that. I have a confession to make." Troy paused before going to open the door. "When we met you were carrying up a bunch of empty beer bottles that you'd gathered on the beach. I was making a joke about writing a book on the anthropological study of modern beach culture and its impact on the environment. I thought I was clever, and I was trying to impress you. Then the next time you asked about it, and I realized you thought I was serious, I wasn't sure how to rewind it."

"So you're not writing an anthropological study of modern beach culture and its impact on the environment?" she asked.

He shook his head in denial. "Not exactly."

"Do you even teach college?" Vivien arched a brow and studied him. She didn't get a lying vibe off him. Were her psychic senses that far off? And was this how non-psychic people felt when they interacted with each other? All this uncertainty?

"Yes. I teach college classes."

"Then is there a reason you don't own a car? I had assumed the reason was you were into the environment."

"I never needed one. I always lived in places with public transportation. Or I bike."

"What are you doing here if not writing about tourist impact on the beach?"

"I needed a change," he said. "So I'm piloting a

program to move more classes online, writing the lessons, modifying the in-class curriculum to work for distance learning, deciding what needs to be in a video format instead of written. If it works, and it should, I'll be able to work from anywhere."

"So you're what? A techie?"

"Somewhat." Troy smiled.

If this were anyone else, she would have been able to sense all of that. With Troy there was an air of mystery. She picked up psychic whispers about him —he was a decent guy, he was attracted to her, he would want commitment over a one-night stand—but that was all.

"Where are you from?" she asked, testing her senses. Maybe somewhere north?

"Colorado, originally," he answered.

"And not originally?"

"I've lived in Oregon, California, Nebraska, here."

Oregon was in the northern United States. Not the north she'd been thinking about when the word popped in her head, but north. "And you teach what? Proust?"

Troy moved past her and finally opened the door. He'd left it unlocked so didn't need a key.

"Yes, a few times, but mostly I teach core

curriculum classes." He gestured for her to go inside. "Did this just turn into a job interview?"

"Interrogation," Vivien retorted as she moved past him to go inside.

She'd seen the home when it had been inhabited by past renters. Troy's decorating choices were non-existent. Just beyond the entryway, he had textbooks piled on the floor next to the couch, flat-screen television on a stand, and a charging laptop on the coffee table next to a remote. It appeared as if he worked in the living room.

Cardboard moving boxes were stacked neatly in a corner. Someone had written on them in permanent marker, *"kitchen," "clothes," "novels."*

"An interrogation, eh?" He laughed. "Carry on, then, detective. I promise I'm not a criminal. I even paid off all my parking tickets."

"How many parking tickets?" Vivien queried.

"Two in the last five years. The meter ran out," he said. "I have no excuse. I lost track of time and forgot to check it."

"But you don't have a car."

"I used to. I sold it."

"Girlfriends?"

"Yes, I've had girlfriends. No, I do not currently have one."

"Wife?"

"An ex-wife."

"Children?"

"My son is in Colorado, getting his undergraduate degree in park administration. He's very outdoorsy. He wants to be a park ranger. His mother and I are very proud of him."

"So one child?"

"Yes, one."

"And how fresh is the divorce?"

"Not so fresh. We had joint custody for most of my son's life. We get along fine now. We never really fought, but we had our moments of tension." He crossed his arms over his chest, and she had the impression he would grow weary of her questioning very soon. "What is it you're trying to figure out?"

Vivien hesitated, not sure how to answer.

"I answered your questions. Answer mine," he said.

"Widowed once. We were young. Cancer. Divorced once. We were stupid, and it wasn't love. No children. I like kids, but motherhood wasn't in my tarot cards." She realized the door was still open behind her, and she leaned to push it closed.

"That wasn't my question," he said. "What is it you're trying to figure out?"

"I'm trying to figure out what I think about this." She gestured her hand back and forth between them.

"Ah." Troy nodded. "I think I understand."

"You do?"

"Sure. You're waiting for a feeling," he answered.

"Yes." Vivien nodded.

"Like the woman in the elevator. You knew that man would ask her to share a ride with him. You had a feeling about it."

She nodded again.

"And that you and your friends were doing spell casting in your living room." He laughed at her stunned expression. "The whole book-candle-set-up kind of gave it away. Plus I walked past the Warrick Theater after you told me about it and read the plaque out front. Your friend's grandmother was a medium. It didn't take much to put two and two together."

"You..." She stepped closer to him, studying him as she tried to discern if he were making fun of her. "You believe me?"

"That you're intuitive? Yes." Troy nodded. "Why wouldn't I believe you?"

Vivien waited for more of a reaction.

"Why are you looking at me like that?" He gave

her a quizzical smile. "I'm not intuitive. You will have to tell me what you're thinking."

"My ancestors worked for carnivals, telling fortunes, reading tarot cards, divining the future. The females in my family all had a gift." Vivien paused and concentrated on him, trying to find the psychic threads that would connect them, but they seemed blocked when it came to Troy. If she couldn't see the threads, she couldn't listen to his secrets. "It is the same gift I have. My grandmother taught me how to see what is not readily known."

Troy nodded. "Cool."

"I'm telling you I'm psychic," Vivien clarified. "That's how I could tell what would happen after that woman left the elevator."

"Okay."

"Cool? Okay? That's it?" She moved closer.

Why couldn't she read him?

"I won't pretend to know how you do it. Maybe you automatically read micro-expressions. Maybe a part of your brain is overdeveloped. Maybe you have magic powers. I don't know, so I can't judge. Until you prove you can't be trusted, I see no reason not to trust what you tell me."

"You're not a very skeptical person, are you?"

This was driving her to distraction. She should pick up more from him than she was.

"Can't you tell what I am feeling?" he asked.

"That's just it. No. Not really. Not clearly." She lifted her hands to cup his cheeks and stared into his dark eyes. Her fingertips brushed over the hints of gray at his temples.

He didn't stop her from touching him. "No, I tend to give people the benefit of the doubt. You telling me that you are intuitive and—"

"Psychic," she inserted. "Clairsentient and claircognizant, to be exact."

"Psychic," he corrected. "You telling me that you are psychic doesn't harm me in any way. So I feel no reason to be distrustful. Though, if you're going to charge me for a reading, I have to tell you, I'm not in the market."

"I don't do that," Vivien said.

"I was teasing," he whispered. "I really do have to get better with my jokes. I promise, normally I am much funnier."

Vivien wasn't a stranger to simple animalistic attraction, but when she stood close to Troy, she felt it vibrating through her core. It wasn't just the stirring desire in her hips, or the fluttering in her stomach, or the ache of her lips and breasts. Sure, all that happened, but she felt it in her toes as they curled in her shoes. It was the nape of her neck longing to be touched. It was her ear wanting to hear his breath whispering past it.

She might not be able to read him like she could others, but she felt him deeply.

"Is it clearer now?" His eyes dipped to her mouth before darting back up to meet her gaze.

"No." Vivien didn't need her psychic abilities to know that she wanted to kiss him. In some ways, not being able to predict what he was about to do and say added an element of fun to the encounter.

He leaned closer. Her hands slid from his cheeks to his chest. "How about now?"

Vivien's lips parted, but only a soft breath came out as she shook her head in denial.

A hand touched her cheek as he ran his thumb along her bottom lip. "Surely it is clearer now?"

Her heartbeat quickened. Here she was, a woman in her forties feeling like she was some foolish teenager about to have her first kiss. In many ways it was ridiculous, and yet here she was, both nervous and excited at the same time.

Troy leaned closer. His lips brushed hers in a soft kiss. She felt him try to pull back but followed him to deepen the contact. Their lips moved in unison only to part and then rejoin as if they each tested the other's resolve.

Vivien leaned into him. She let her hands explore his shoulders and arms and up to his neck. When he touched her, she didn't know where his hands would roam. They lightly trailed down her sides to rest on her hips.

"How about now?" he asked.

"I think I'm getting a sharper picture," she answered. "A tour of your house might help?"

"You want to see my..." He glanced around the room.

"Bedroom," she clarified.

"Oh, right." He took her hand and led her down a hall to an opened door. The bed was small compared to hers, and paperback novels were stacked inside the headboard shelves. A magazine rested on the unmade bedspread.

Troy let go of her hand and swept the magazine onto the floor. He pulled on the covers but stopped when she touched his shoulder.

"We're only going to mess it up," she said.

Vivien liked that this was not the room of a man who expected female company. Though messy, it was not dirty. She appreciated that as well.

She reached for the buttons on her shirt, unfastening them as he watched. The blouse slipped off her arms. He eagerly pulled his t-shirt over his head and dropped it on the floor.

Vivien kicked off her shoes and pushed her pants from her hips. When she stood before him in a pink lace bra and panties, she paused as he looked at her.

"I, ah..." He appeared at a loss for words. "Oh, crap, hold on."

Vivien inhaled sharply in surprise as he rushed from the room. She stood, stunned, as the sounds of his footsteps ran away from her.

"Troy?" she called after him, confused.

Well, she hadn't seen that one coming. She reached for her shirt. A loud bang sounded from somewhere in the house, and she started to thread her arm through the sleeve.

Footsteps sounded again, and Troy appeared in the doorway. He held up a condom packet. "Found one."

Vivien let he sleeve fall from her wrist. Troy tossed the condom on the bed and unbuttoned his jeans. As he stripped from his clothing, she crawled onto the bed. When she again looked at him, the need he felt for her was undeniable. She tugged a bra strap off her shoulder to free a breast.

Troy crawled over her, kissing his way along her

leg, up her thigh, pausing near her hip, and then venturing up the valley of her breasts.

Vivien lifted her hips and pushed the panties down her legs. They worked in tandem to strip her of the last pieces of clothing. The desire ran deep, and she eagerly parted her legs for him.

Troy kissed her as he put the condom on. The first cool brush of latex along her thigh soon warmed.

Vivien had always been a woman who knew what she wanted. She pushed Troy onto his back, letting her thighs straddle him. She worked her hips until his body was in line to enter hers.

He let her have complete control as she lowered herself onto him. His moans revealed how much he enjoyed the rhythm she set. The feelings she had around him simmered to the surface until each brush of skin moved them closer to the brink.

When her release came, it was almost a surprise. It shook her deeply as she trembled and jerked. Troy groaned, gripping her hips tight as he too met his climax.

Vivien leaned over, breathing hard as the pleasure rolled through her entire body.

"Oh, wow," Troy mumbled as if stunned by what had transpired between them. "I mean, like, wow."

"I'll take that as a compliment." She moved to lie

next to him on the bed. As she settled onto her back, she turned her head to look at him.

"Most definitely," he answered, still breathless. "I'm not sure what I said or did, but if you could please tell me so I can repeat it in the future, that'd be great. Until you showed up tonight, I wasn't even sure you liked me."

"Glad I could clear that up for you," she teased. "Maybe you can clear something up for me?"

"What's that?"

"When you said you found one, was it really only one?" Vivien grinned and rolled onto her side to better look at him. "Or am I spending the night so we can do that again?"

CHAPTER ELEVEN

VIVIEN KNEW she wasn't in her own bed before she opened her eyes. It didn't feel like her mattress or her sheets. She felt a leg stir, and a muscular calf bumped into hers. A hand rested next to her naked hip, the fingers unmoving. The heat of his body and the gentle pressure of his touch against her skin focused her attention.

Troy.

She had been tipsy when she came over, but not so much that she'd blame anything on the liquor. This was her decision, and one she did not regret. She shifted her hip so that it pressed more fully into his hand. His fingers twitched against her.

Vivien smiled. This kind of intimacy was new,

and in many ways, better than sex—and she enjoyed sex. For all her experiences in life, waking up with a man hadn't happened often outside of her two marriages. That meant something.

What was it that Heather had said to her?

"You are allowed to love more than one person in your life. You can have two great loves. You can have three, or four, or a dozen. And in doing so, you're not betraying those who came before. Love isn't like that. You don't get a finite amount of it."

Is that what this was? Love? It felt like it to her.

To most people, to say they were in love after such a brief period would be insanity. Vivien wasn't most people. Whereas others were mired in self-doubt, she trusted her feelings—usually. She wasn't perfect. She'd made mistakes and terrible decisions. Rex proved that. But she also had the benefit of seeing parts of the bigger picture that were often missed.

Vivien did not fall in love easily. The torch she carried for Sam proved that. Twenty years was a long time. But, before now, if she hadn't met the right person, the one who shook her to the core, then her belief that there was only Sam had never been challenged.

She studied Troy as he slept next to her. His heavy breath came from his parted lips.

"You are allowed to love more than one person in your life."

Another memory countered Heather's words.

"Save your heart for me. It's mine."

Vivien suppressed a yawn. It was way too early in the morning for all this reflection.

Coffee. She needed coffee.

She eased off the bed, careful not to jar Troy awake. She gathered her clothes off the floor and took them to the hallway where she dressed, except for her shoes, which she carried.

Her tour of the home had been limited the evening before, but she had been in the house when there had been previous tenants. She knew where the rooms were located.

"If I was coffee, where would I hide?" she whispered as she entered Troy's kitchen. Seeing a coffee pot on the countertop, she started for it.

"Viv?"

The word was soft. She smiled as she turned to answer Troy. "Hey, I was just..."

He wasn't there.

"Troy?" She walked to the doorway and made her way to the living room. The house was quiet.

Maybe she'd imagined it.

She turned to go back to the coffee pot.

"Viv."

The sound came from directly behind her. Her hand tingled from the ring on her forefinger. She slowly turned.

The living room was empty. The laptop on his coffee table was closed. The television was off.

She moved toward the door, glancing at the window to see if someone was outside.

"Viv."

The sound was louder than before and came from the couch.

She froze, her eyes widening as she turned to look. Sam sat on the couch. His transparent body had filled in, and he was more substantial than before. He didn't look like a ghost, at least none of the versions she'd seen. The difference was subtle, but it was there.

He lifted his hand, smiling.

"Sam? How?"

"Viv." The word formed by his lips didn't move. The image of him blipped like the skip of an old movie reel that had been sliced and repaired. He again lifted his hand in the same gesture, smiling.

The moment felt familiar as if this were some

memory she projected onto Troy's furniture. Was this what a mental break felt like?

She moved closer to him, lifting her hand as she reached to touch him. "Sam?"

"Viv." The image blipped, and he repeated the same actions.

"What is this?" she asked, sitting next to him on the couch. She let her hand hover near his face but was afraid to make contact.

"Viv." He reset himself and smiled toward where she had been standing moments before.

"I don't..." She frowned. "I'm not doing anything wrong. This is my subconscious mind working out some weird stress and guilt, but I know logically I have no reason to feel guilty."

"Viv." Sam waved and smiled at nothing.

"You look so young," she said. "When I think about you, I always forget just how young we were."

"Viv."

"This isn't real." Vivien finally got up the nerve to touch the figure. Energy poured out of her ring finger the moment she made contact. She tried to pull away, but it was too late.

Sam dropped his hand and turned to look at her. Awareness filled his eyes. She became frozen in place.

MICHELLE M. PILLOW

"Hey, baby." He grinned. "Want to go down to the beach today?"

Vivien shook her head in denial. The flow of energy built in her fingertips until she felt the warmth of flesh. His face became solid.

"What's the matter, Viv? You look like you've seen a ghost. Your super senses activating again?" She'd forgotten the exact tone of his voice, and that he'd called her psychic abilities "super senses" like it was some kind of superhuman power.

"You can't be here, Sam. You have to go." Vivien glanced toward Troy's bedroom, not wanting to wake him. How could she explain this? "We said goodbye. I should never have tried to bring you back to me. I wanted to recapture that feeling I had when I was with you. When we were young and stupid and so in love. I know what we had is in the past. It was tough to let go. I will always love you. And I know you will always love me. Maybe someday we will see each other again, but this can't happen now. I can't go to the beach with you."

Sam began humming softly. It wasn't lost on her that a week ago she would have given anything for this moment, but now she knew she needed to move on. It had been too long. She wasn't the same girl

Sam had fallen in love with. She'd been holding on to a dream.

"There is only us," he sang, his voice nearly a whisper. "Only our hearts. I'll be watching you."

"Sam, stop," Vivien insisted.

Sam's image blipped.

"Viv." He again waved and smiled at nothing.

"Vivien? Are you still here?" Troy called, his sleepy voice coming from the direction of his bedroom.

Sam turned to her and winked. "See you later, baby."

"Vivien?" Troy inquired.

"Save your heart for me. It's mine."

"Uh, yeah, here." She rubbed her eyes even though tears didn't fall. Sam's presence had left her feeling drained.

Troy appeared in a pair of loose pajama pants and nothing else. Seeing her, he smiled. "Did I catch you trying to sneak out?"

Vivien stood from the couch. "I was about to get coffee."

"I have coffee." He eagerly went toward the kitchen. She heard him rummaging around.

Vivien had the impression he wanted to please her. The psychic intuition wasn't as detailed as she was used to, but it was more than she had been getting around him.

She went to the kitchen door, focusing on picking up anything she could. Thoughts of Sam lingered. His appearance confused her. At first he'd looked like a projection of her subconscious, but then he'd spoken, and that felt more like his spirit. Was he real or a manifestation of guilt?

Troy scooped coffee into a filter. He glanced over his shoulder at her. "Strong or very strong or heart-exploding?"

"Strong and lots of sugar," she answered, feeling like her blood sugar was low. That was another sign her new magic had been used.

Troy dumped some of the grounds back into the container to lessen the strength before starting the brewing process. "Would you like eggs?"

"No, thank you. Just the coffee."

Troy pulled mugs out of a cabinet before grabbing a small bag of sugar. "Are you sure? I'm pretty good at cooking eggs. It's kind of my specialty."

"I'm not sure I have time this morning, but maybe next time?"

At that he smiled. The look reached all the way into his eyes. He came across the kitchen to stand in front of her. "I like that there will be a next time. I'm still not sure how there was a first time. I didn't think you liked me much, but I'm not complaining. I'm happy to be wrong."

"We women are mysterious creatures," Vivien said. "Don't try to figure us out."

"I wouldn't dare." Troy leaned over to kiss the corner of her mouth. His lips stayed closed, and the contact was brief.

He went to pour the coffee from the pot before it was down brewing. He put one of the coffee mugs under the brewing stream as he filled the other with the pot.

"There you go," he said. "Coffee as promised. I'll let you do the sugar this first time."

Vivien joined him by the coffee pot and poured sugar from the bag directly into her cup.

Troy chuckled. "You do like sugar."

"Not normally this much," she said. "I need a little extra kick today."

That was an understatement.

She took a sip of the coffee and tried not to think of Sam showing up in Troy's living room. "What are your plans for the day?"

"Actually, I have to put on a suit and go pretend to be a movie star." He pulled the coffee mug out from under the hot stream of brewing coffee and replaced it with the pot.

Vivien laughed. "Tell me you're not talking about the indie film down at the beach with all those women in bikinis. You're in that?"

Troy shook his head. "Wrong kind of suit." He suddenly chuckled. "And very wrong kind of film. I found a high school kid with a camera, and he's going to record a series of lectures for me on your favorite author."

"John Grisham?"

"Proust," Troy corrected.

"Ah, yes, good ole Proust." Sarcastically, she added in a playful voice, "I am so sorry I will miss that. If I could be there, I would."

"You weren't invited." He made a show of drinking his coffee. "I need the students listening to me, not daydreaming about the hot chick at my side hanging on my every word."

She gave a dramatic sigh. "I guess I'll have to go see if the beach movie has any room for a hot chick."

Troy gave a small moan and bit his lip. He pretended to look her over. "If you will be running around in a bikini all day, I might have to blow off the Audio-Visual Club's president and come watch you work instead."

"Ah, poor AV club guy." She started to laugh, but a feeling came over her and she added, "He'll need this for his college resume. Be sure to give him an excellent letter of recommendation for his file."

"I didn't think to offer that. Good idea. Thanks," he said. "Now, if I can't get you to watch me get my Proust on, I will try to tempt you with the beginner's algebra class tomorrow."

"Oh, algebra." She pretended to shiver. "You sure do know how to show a girl a good time."

"Then an introductory segment for beginning psychology, some troubleshooting tutorials on using the new system, and a lesson on beach geography for an Earth science chapter."

"And here I thought I lived on the wild side." She ran her finger along the edge of her mug before tapping her finger on the coffee's surface to watch it ripple. "I thought you professors usually stuck to one department."

"Normally, yes, but I'm special."

"Ah, I see. Of course."

"What about you? Any crazy plans for the day?"

"I need to head out of town for work," she answered. "It will be incredibly boring."

"What do you do? I don't think you ever said. I

would have asked about that out on the first date, but we skipped ahead."

"I don't do much," she said.

He set his mug down. "Are you really not going to tell me?"

"I own a few fast food restaurants in the area," she said.

"What's a few?"

"Twenty-seven."

"You own twenty-seven restaurants?" he repeated in disbelief.

"And some commercial properties," she admitted. This wasn't something she typically talked about. It was no one's business how she made her money. Some people in town had an inkling she owned a few franchises or managed them for a group of investors. Others assumed she lived off Rex's alimony payments. "I have a gift for sensing if a location will be profitable or not. I also have a knack for hiring the right people to manage them."

"Wait, so the taco truck that you showed me? Is that you?"

"Oh, I wish." She put her mug down on the counter next to his. "I have been trying to convince Maria to franchise. She won't come off her secrets."

"I had absolutely no idea I was living next door to

a restaurateur." He let his finger dance along her arm in light caresses.

"I'm glad you're impressed by my quarter pound hamburgers and chicken nuggets." She placed her hand on his chest. "I should get going."

"Will I see you later?" he asked. "I'd really like to."

"Maybe. Have a pen? I'll leave you my cell, and you can text me after you're done with your filming. I'm not sure where I'll be or how long it will take." Her hand dropped from him as he moved to a drawer. He placed a pen and paper on the counter for her. As she scrolled down her number, she said, "And don't play coy and wait forty-eight hours or whatever time allotment is considered cool to call me. I hate that."

"I don't think I've ever been accused of being cool before." He cupped her cheek. "But I promise. No games. There is something about you, Vivien Stone. I want this to work between us."

"I know." She nodded. That fact was one of the few things she'd picked up from him the first time they'd met. He was a man of commitment.

"You know?"

"I'm psychic, remember." She leaned forward to kiss him. "Thank you for the coffee."

"Thank you for the..." He grinned as if stopping himself from saying something inappropriate.

"You're welcome." She winked at him, gave him another quick kiss, and then turned to go. She leaned over to pick up her shoes from the living room floor and glanced at the empty couch before leaving.

CHAPTER TWELVE

Vivien didn't technically have to spend the day visiting properties, but she wanted to get away from Freewild Cove and could think of nothing better than being alone in her car. Music played, muted by the sound of wind whipping through her windows. Heather had wanted to come with her. Vivien had refused the company but promised to stay in contact. She needed to contemplate her current feelings, and she couldn't do that when she kept absorbing her friends' emotions each time they bumped into each other.

Besides, Lorna was starting back at work. Vivien preferred Heather to be near Lorna if anything happened. Not that she thought anything would happen. The feeling of dread she'd picked up in the theater before the smudging had disappeared. Lorna would be safe. The best thing was for life to get back to normal for all three of them. Magic was fun, but they still had jobs to do. For Vivien, that meant a lot of employees who depended on her.

Her cell phone rang, and Vivien pushed the button on the steering wheel to answer it without bothering to look to see who it was.

"Hello, you got Vivien."

"Vivien?" Rex's voice was the last one she expected to hear, though she realized she shouldn't have been surprised. When she didn't bother to call him after that day in his office, he would have started to panic. In truth, she barely thought about it. Her mind had been focused elsewhere.

She frowned. "Hello, Rex."

"How are you?" His words were cheery, too cheery.

"I'm busy," she answered between clenched teeth. "What's up?"

"I wanted to apologize for Harry's behavior the other day," he said. "I understand why you were upset. He didn't present himself very well."

Harry's behavior?

Yeah, right. Harry. It was all Harry.

"All right," she said. The green countryside

rolled past her, but she kept her eyes on the road. Rex made her tired. Ever since their divorce, he was like talking to a psychic vampire. He always wanted something and acted like she should want to give it to him.

"He thought he was doing what I wanted, but I never wanted him to insult you. I don't think he explained himself well though." Rex tried to keep his tone light. "Next time, it will be just you and me talking."

"Will it? I don't know. Harry made it sound like I needed to get my lawyer involved. I don't feel comfortable renegotiating legally binding contracts without my council. I'm sure you understand." She toyed with the idea of just hanging up on him. Knowing Rex, he'd just keep calling back. She might as well let him get to whatever point he was moving toward.

"That's why I called. I don't think there is any reason to get the courts involved. We're both reasonable adults. I think we can work this out between us."

If she had been physically able to punch a voice, she would have pounded the shit out of his placating tone.

"I'm not sure what there is to work out, Rex," she mimicked his overly fake manner. "We have a contract. You offered me that contract. I took it. I want to honor it, and you want to take me to court."

"I don't want to take you to court," he said.

She already knew that. She had one horribly long video reason why he didn't want this to get ugly. "That's not what Harry said."

She was being obtuse on purpose, but he deserved to squirm a little.

"Harry misspoke," Rex insisted.

"He seemed sure. He had a folder and everything." She drifted to the right as a giant semi-truck came down the two-lane highway a little too close to the centerline. "Three folders, actually."

"Viv, I'm perfectly willing to honor our original deal. I want to take care of you."

She opened her mouth wide and had to fight the urge to gag.

"I'm just asking if you would please sign an amendment making it clear that we agreed to thirty-five percent of my income at the time of our divorce," he continued. "Really, it's to make the bookkeeping easier on everyone. That way you don't have to worry about audits, and paying lawyers to dig around, or if I get demoted and start earning less. I'm thinking about you here. Clarity is good business."

Did he think she'd buy what he was shoveling

right now? She already assumed he was skimming off the top. She was sure there was creative accounting going on. The irony of the whole situation was, if he'd just asked her nicely without threats or pretense, she would have signed the damned agreement locking in the thirty-five percent.

"I wouldn't feel right taking the same amount if you were demoted," Vivien denied, feigning concern. "I couldn't do that to *you*. Let's keep the agreement the way it is for the sake of simplicity."

"But—"

"I insist."

"Okay, but—"

"Was there something else?" she asked.

His tone lowered, losing all traces of his forced charm. "You remember that you can't show people that video, right?"

And there it was.

"As long as I'm not forced to, I promise I won't," she said. "That video embarrasses me as much as it does you."

That was truer when they first split up, less so now.

"And you're not going to take me to court for forty percent?"

"As long as I'm not forced to," she repeated.

"And the audit?" Rex insisted. "Now that I explained that Harry was mistaken, you're not going to audit the firm, are you?"

"I haven't decided yet." She hadn't given it much thought. "As long as I don't feel a reason to. Harry was pretty threatening. I don't want to talk to him again without my lawyer there. Make sure he knows that."

She was about eighty percent certain Harry and the other partners were listening to the call. Tiny noises sounded behind Rex's voice.

"I think you'll be pleasantly surprised with your next deposit," he said.

"I'm sure I will." It only mattered because of the charities she sent monthly donations to with the funds. "If there's nothing else, Rex, I'm about to walk into an appointment."

"No, there's nothing else. Thanks for being so understanding, Viv. You looked great the other day by the way."

"Goodbye, Rex." She didn't give him a chance to say anything else as she pushed the button on her steering wheel to end the call.

It took her several deep breaths before she could concentrate past the lines on the road. Rex was more of a nuisance than anything else. It wasn't surprising that he'd called to make sure she wasn't talking to her lawyer to take him to court. He knew he'd messed up. Making him sweat about it would only prolong her interactions with him.

She passed a sign saying her exit was in five miles, and then a billboard for one of her restaurants. It looked a little faded, and she made a mental note to talk to the advertising company that handled it.

"That's who you married after me?"

Vivien cried out in surprise as Sam's voice came from directly behind her. The car swerved, and the tires ran into the ditch. Her heart leaped into her throat. She jerked the wheel to correct the car's trajectory.

Vivien made it back onto the road, but the over-correction took her across the opposite lane. A semi-trunk honked a warning, and it barely missed striking her back end. She slammed on the brakes, stopping the vehicle along the wrong side of the road. Her hands shook and took the car out of gear. She took several deep breaths.

"No offense, babe, but he sounds like a loser," Sam continued as if nothing had happened.

Vivien looked in the rearview mirror but didn't see him. She turned around to find him lounging in the back. His feet were on the seat and his back against the door. She could see the seat through his body.

"Sam, what the hell?" she demanded, her tone harsh after the fright he'd given her. "You can't pop up behind me like that. You almost got me killed!"

He reached over his head and picked at the seal along the window as if bored. His fingers had no effect on her car. "When did you get so serious? I remember you putting your hands over my eyes when I was driving. You told me to feel the road."

She had done that once. Those had been crazy, wild times. "That was stupid of me. I shouldn't have."

Vivien studied him. His body contorted into a position that caused her back to spasm just looking at it. Sam looked so young, younger than the image she had carried with her. His handsome boyish face hadn't gained in years, and his eyes lacked the wisdom that only came with age and experience. She didn't get the impression that he wanted her dead, but then, their track record on the subject wasn't great.

"Sam, you know that I don't want to die, right?" she insisted. "You can't keep trying to lure me to my death."

"Why would I try to do that?"

"Then what are you doing here?" she asked. "You can't be here. I know I séanced you but—"

"What are any of us doing here, Viv?" He stared at her as he pushed up from the door. "Let's go to the beach. You love the beach."

A knock on her window caused her to jump in her seat. She spun around to find a highway patrolman gesturing that she should roll down the glass for him.

Vivien glanced behind her only to find Sam was gone.

"Hello, ma'am," he stated. "What seems to be the problem here?"

There was no way on Earth she was answering that question truthfully.

"Bee," she lied as she turned off the engine.

He leaned over the look inside her car. "I'll need to see your license, registration, and proof of insurance."

"Yes, sir." Vivien leaned over to the glove box to retrieve the registration and insurance before digging in her purse for her wallet. Sam had startled her, and she forced herself to focus on the patrolman so she could read him and get out of a ticket. She handed all three items over to him.

"Have you been drinking ma'am?"

"Just coffee." She smiled. "Maybe a little too much."

He didn't laugh at her lame joke. "Is there a reason you're parked on this side of the road?"

Vivien knew this man was used to people lying to him and making up excuses in an effort to get out of tickets. All he wanted was for someone to take responsibility for their mistakes and poor judgments. Her best bet was honesty... to a point. "I became startled, nearly drove off the road, overcorrected, and ended up here. I was trying to catch my breath after almost colliding with a semi-truck. I'm just thankful that no one was hurt by my mistake."

He stood and glanced over the top of her car. When he again looked down at her, he said, "That seems consistent with your tire tracks. Wait here."

Vivien waited before he was away, before she said, "Sam, you can't keep showing up. We sent you on in peace. You should be in the light. Go find the light."

She couldn't be sure, but she thought she heard the faint sound of a guitar answering her. The music was cut off as a semi-truck rumbled past.

Vivien rubbed the bridge of her nose. Checking on the restaurant properties was going to have to wait. She needed to get home and deal with her dead first husband.

"Here you go, ma'am." The patrolman handed the license through the window. "I will let you off with a warning but try to be more careful. These trucks can't make quick stops. You're lucky you weren't badly injured or worse."

"I will. Thank you, sir." She started to smile, but he turned away before she could say more.

"Have a good day, ma'am." His words flowed behind him like an afterthought.

CHAPTER THIRTEEN

SAM KEPT TRYING to get her to the beach.

He'd attempted to lure her to the water the first night. Next, he'd waved at her to follow him. He might have tried to get her there again. Now, he just flat out asked.

What if Sam hadn't been trying to kill her? What if her first instincts about him were right? What was at the beach that he wanted her to see so badly?

The idea wouldn't leave her, so she determined that there must be a reason she kept coming back to it, like an itch that needed to be scratched. Heather always said that ghosts were often confused and had trouble communicating. Sometimes their messages were hard to hear and decipher. Sam had a substantial amount of morphine in his system when he died.

What if that lingered in death? What if that was why Vivien had felt pill drunk, as Lorna has so eloquently put it?

Vivien drove slowly with both hands on the wheel. She kept the music off, refused to answer her phone, and continuously glanced over her shoulder to see if Sam would come back. Once, she even pulled over to let a caravan of semi-trucks pass. Intentional or not, the series of near-death experiences had left her jittery.

When she finally turned off the engine in the driveway of her home, she took a deep breath of relief. She sat for a moment, staring out the windshield toward the path that would take her to the beach. She wasn't sure what she'd find, if anything, out there.

Fear whispered that she shouldn't go. She needed to be smart and safe.

Psychic intuition told her Sam would never try to hurt her.

Her growing magical powers warned that she didn't have enough information on what was happening.

Logic said, if she were going to go to the beach, she needed to take Lorna and Heather with her. They could watch in case she acted strangely.

She couldn't ask Troy. How in the world did she explain to her new man-friend that she was being haunted by her dead husband from twenty years ago? Oh, and furthermore that she was the one who'd summoned him, so it was her fault that Sam was hanging around? Or that her family legend dictated she had only one soul mate and sorry, it could never be Troy because she'd already had Sam?

"Sam? Are you here?" She glanced at the empty back seat. He didn't answer.

Vivien looked at Troy's house. She wanted to see him but knew he was probably filming his teaching segments. Images of him played in her mind—holding the coffee cup out to her in the morning, the questioning smile bathed in the sunlight coming through the car window as they drove to the taco truck, the worry on his face after he'd pulled her from the water, his shadowed features while he'd slept.

Troy had lived. He had experiences and wisdom that shone in his eyes and were etched in his handsome face. She couldn't say where the relationship was heading, but she wanted to find out.

"There is only us." Sam's voice whispered through her thoughts, and she wasn't sure whether it were real or just the same memory that had haunted

her since his last breath. Was it meant to make her feel guilty about the feelings she had for Troy?

"Only our hearts," she answered the thought.

"I'll be watching you. Save your heart for me. It's mine."

"Okay, Sam, okay. You win. I'll go to the beach." She opened the car door. "But I'm not going alone."

Vivien grabbed her purse and her cell phone. Her fingers moved automatically to call Heather. Her friend answered before she made it to the front door.

"Hey, I was just thinking about calling you," Heather said. "I'm not sure why. I just felt... I don't know. Something. What's up?"

"I need you to come to the beach with me. Sam's back. I think he wants to show me something." Vivien stuck her key in the lock, but the door opened before she could touch the knob.

"You're home," Lorna said before she saw Vivien carried a phone. She covered her mouth as if to stop herself from interrupting further.

"It's Heather." Vivien turned on the speakerphone. "Heather, Lorna's here too. We're at the house. Can you come?"

"Good, stay with Lorna. Let me tell these guys

I'm leaving and I'll be there in fifteen." Heather hung up.

"What's happening?" Lorna asked. She stepped aside as Vivien came inside the house.

"Sam showed up in my back seat when I was driving. He startled me and I nearly ran into oncoming traffic." Vivien tossed her purse and cell phone on the couch cushion. "I think we had it wrong. He's not trying to hurt me. I think in his confused spirit way, he is trying to get me to go to the beach. Maybe that's where he wants to say goodbye."

The smell of pastries filled the home, catching her attention.

"Did you bake?" Vivien automatically moved toward the kitchen.

"I had William run me by the grocery store and I stocked up on a few things for us." Lorna followed her. "I made an apple pie. It just came out of the oven."

"So you did." Vivien went to the fresh pie on her stove and leaned over to smell. The warmth drifted up to her face. Lorna had cut little decorations in the crust. "This looks as good as any bakery I've been to, actually better."

Vivien went to the fridge and peeked inside.

Lorna had completely stocked it. "You weren't kidding."

"I'm not sure it's safe for you to go to the beach," Lorna picked up the conversation as if Vivien hadn't been sidetracked by the smell of food. "We should try summoning Sam here, or at the theater."

"I think it needs to be at the beach." Vivien shut the fridge door. "I can't explain how I know, but I just feel it. He keeps trying to get me to follow him there. If you don't want to come, I'll understand. I don't want you to put yourself in danger."

"There is no way I'm letting you go without me," Lorna denied. She went to the cupboard and pulled out three plates and set them on the counter close to the cooling pie. "The three of us are stronger together. I owe you and Heather so much."

Vivien pulled three forks, a knife, and a pie server out of a drawer. She handed them to Lorna.

"Heather gave me a job when I had nothing." Lorna cut the pie into equal slices. "You gave me a place to live when I couldn't remain in my apartment. Without both of you, I would still be locked in misery over Glenn's betrayal. You helped me say goodbye to him, and I was able to then let go of the past."

Lorna dished up the three plates and carried

them into the living room, overlapping the edges of two of the plates so she could carry them with one hand like a waitress. She set them on the coffee table. Vivien followed her.

"You encouraged me to say yes to William," Lorna continued, "and I have never been happier. After everything you have done for me, there is no way I will abandon you when it's time for you to find your peace. Whatever you want, whatever you need, I'm here for you."

Vivien nodded, touched by Lorna's words. Her voice was soft as she answered, "I want Troy."

Lorna smiled and nodded. "We know. We felt it after you came home with tacos."

"Part of me feels like I should feel guilty, you know?" Vivien continued. "But I don't, so then I feel guilty about not feeling guilty. Somewhere along the way I'd become stuck on the idea of Sam. I'd been told my entire life that women in my family only get one shot at love. If that love died, then we were cursed never to have it again. I really believed that, but then I met Troy and..."

"The world shifted?" Lorna supplied.

Vivien frowned. "Why did you phrase it like that?"

Her grandmother had always described meeting her true love in those terms.

Lorna shook her head and shrugged. "I don't know. It was the only way I could think to describe the feeling I picked up from you."

"I never thought it was possible, but maybe Heather is right. Maybe you can have more than one love of your life. Sam will always have a place in my heart, but Troy, he's..."

Lorna gently rubbed Vivien's upper back. "I know."

Vivien didn't know how to finish the sentence. Troy was here. He was her age and maturity level. He gave her something she'd been missing for years. He was the future, possibilities, her next chapter. Maybe the feelings weren't meant to be put into words.

"But Sam is..." Vivien lifted her hand helplessly to the sides.

"I know," Lorna said. "I think you're trying to come up with a simple answer in a complicated situation, but I will say you are allowed to be happy."

The door opened, and Heather rushed inside. "What did you mean when you said Sam is back, and are you all right?"

Heather looked around the home as if she could

find the answer about Sam for herself.

"Yes, I'm all right," Vivien assured her. "I think I know what he wants me to do."

"She needs us to go to the beach with her," Lorna put forth. "There is no way she should go alone."

Vivien explained all that had happened, so everyone was on the same page.

Heather nodded. "I should have insisted you stay home today."

"I should have stayed home with you," Lorna added.

"Have you ever known me not to live my life?" Vivien asked, more of Heather since Lorna was a newer friendship. "I've followed my psychic instincts since the day I was born. I honestly didn't feel like Sam wanted to harm me. If I stop listening to the signs and start living in fear, that is when I'll really be in trouble."

"But the water..." Heather gestured weakly in the direction of the beach. "How can you say that wasn't intentional?"

"I don't have all the answers, but I have to believe in what I feel. If I can't trust myself, then I am not sure how to live," Vivien said.

Heather glanced at the two women and then down at the coffee table.

"That smells fresh," Heather said, pointing at the pie.

"Lorna made it," Vivien said.

"I thought maybe having sugar around might help the cravings after we use our magic. Maybe even if we eat before we séance," Lorna said. "Plus, I like to bake."

"That's a brilliant idea. If we sugar load before a séance, maybe we won't feel so drained after," Heather agreed. "By this logic, it would practically be irresponsible of us not to eat more desserts."

"We do like being responsible adults." Vivien grabbed a plate and sank into a chair.

"It's a hard job, but someone has to eat this pie." Heather sat on the couch and picked up a plate. Lorna joined her.

After several bites, Heather said, "What happened with Troy last night? I have been waiting all day for details. We tried to stay up to see how asking him on a date went, but you didn't come home."

Vivien smiled. "Troy and I... Well, let's just say that he was a surprise—a *very* good surprise."

Ordinarily she would have told her friends everything, but with this story, she decided to leave a few of the details out.

CHAPTER FOURTEEN

SAND PUSHED its way between her toes as Vivien walked barefoot over the beach. The sound of the water lapping against the coast created a backdrop to the distant screams of children playing along the shoreline. Occasionally the murmur of voices from the distant public beach caught on the wind.

Vivien loved the smell of the ocean, the hint of salt and seaweed. Depending on the time of year, the breeze would carry the fragrance of wildflowers from the vegetation along the edge of the sand. Though she couldn't smell the wildflowers today, the strong memory of them tricked her senses and she imagined them lingering in the fresh air.

"The water seems too cold to let children play in

it," Heather said, zipping her lightweight jacket as the breeze coming off the water became stronger.

Vivien had changed into a pair of leggings and layered a long sweater over a t-shirt. She carried her sandals, preferring the feel of the sun-warmed sand beneath her bare feet.

"Do you see him?" Lorna asked, not for the first time. She'd appeared on edge since they left the house as if she were on alert to fight off anything that tried to come near them.

"No," Heather and Vivien answered in unison.

Lorna kept to the wet sand where it was easier to walk in her sneakers.

Heather stayed between them. "Any clue on where we're going or how long until we get there?"

Vivien wasn't sure where they were going. All she knew is that when they walked toward the water where Sam had first led her, she had the urge to turn left and stroll along the slight curve of the inlet. "I have no idea."

"Good thing we brought our phones to call a cab," Lorna said. "If we end up walking another ten miles, there is no way I'm making the journey back."

Heather laughed at the exaggeration. They were scarcely a mile from Vivien's home.

"Is your hip bothering you?" Vivien asked, concerned.

"No, I'm just being dramatic." Lorna said.

As they neared an old walkover, Vivien stopped to study it. The metal had rusted, and the boards had bowed until it appeared less like a functioning walkway and more like the skeletal remains of an ancient serpent, blown from the ocean and smothered in the sand.

"What is it?" Heather asked.

"I'm not sure." Vivien moved quickly toward the structure. The smell of the beach changed, now carrying a hint of decay from the rotted wood. She cut across the beach through the loose sand only to stop near the end of the metal skeleton. The walkover had served as a way to pass over the vegetation leading to the sand and did not make it to the water's edge like a boardwalk. Her friends followed her. "I thought I sensed something, but I don't know."

The wood slats had decayed over time, though a few broken pieces still clung to the metal with old bolts. Someone had nailed a no trespassing sign on a falling rail, but it had faded to the point the lettering was barely decipherable.

"That looks like a great way to catch tetanus," Lorna said. "I wonder why they don't tear it down."

"It's been like this ever since I can remember." Vivien walked toward the structure. "This is it."

"Is what?" Heather asked. "A safety hazard? Yes. We should petition the town council to do something about it."

"No, this is the place." Vivien looked at the water's edge. With the curve of the beach, her home was a straight shot across the choppy waves. She held her arm out straight and pointed the tips of her fingers toward her house. "This is where Sam was trying to take me that first night, only he cut across the water in a straight line. He wasn't trying to drown me. He wanted to lead me here."

"Why here?" Lorna asked. She shaded her eyes as she looked toward the nearest crowd.

Vivien closed her eyes, hearing the ocean. She remembered the sensation of twirling around as Sam spun her until she could no longer stand.

"Viv?" Heather prompted.

"Don't you remember? This is where Sam asked me to marry him." Vivien began to rotate, slowly at first, as she felt her feet shift in the dry sand. She lifted her arms to give her body balance.

"There is only us," he had whispered as he kneeled in the sand. *"Only our hearts. Say you love me. Say you'll be mine forever. Marry me, Viv."*

"Yes," she mouthed. Vivien twirled faster, just as she had that night. Sam had taken her hands and spun her until her heart pounded and she was dizzy.

She leaned back her head and opened her eyes. The sky moved. She imagined she heard laughter. It wasn't long before her rotations became wider, and she stumbled to keep her footing.

Images and sounds of the past swam through her thoughts in no particular order—Sam laughing as he packed their van with blankets, the time they argued over grocery money, running across the street drunk and almost getting hit by a honking car, high school prom, a glance, a kiss, a tear, a scream, the doctor repeating the words they'd been too stunned to hear, and finally that last rattling breath from his chapped lips.

"Uh, Vivien?" Heather said, sounding concerned. "Are you doing that on purpose, or are you possessed? We can't tell."

"There she is." Sam's garbled voice sounded as if from far away. "There's my girl."

Vivien dropped her arms and lowered her head.

She swayed on her feet as her eyes met Sam's. The dizzying effect of spinning made it hard to focus. He seemed more sunlight than man, an almost translucent image of his former self.

"Should we...?" Lorna whispered to Heather in concern.

"Just wait," Heather answered.

"He's here. Do you see him?" Vivien asked, not taking her eyes from Sam.

"Yes," the two women said in unison.

"How in the world are we going to be able to explain this if someone comes by?" Lorna asked. They had discussed the subject at length and had all agreed that none of them were ready to be publicly ousted as a medium. In the era of internet and camera phones, such a revelation would make life unbearable.

"That crowd is pretty far away. I think we're good," Vivien added, even though she didn't turn to look down the beach. She didn't want to take her eyes away from Sam for fear he'd disappear again.

"Yeah, I don't think anyone else can see him," Heather said. "Otherwise we'd be getting a lot more stares right now."

Vivien stared at Sam for what felt like a long time. Deep inside she knew this would be the last time she saw him. A tear slid down her cheek. He seemed content, like a mirage waiting for the sunlight to release it.

"There is only us," he whispered.

"Only our hearts," she answered with a nod.

Heather touched her shoulder from behind. She felt her friend without looking to confirm which one it was. Empathy and concern flowed from Heather into Vivien.

"You have to say goodbye," Heather said. "It's time."

"Sam, I—" Vivien began, but he disappeared. She gasped.

"There." Lorna appeared next to her, pointing. "He's there."

Sam had rematerialized near the end of the metal skeleton. He pointed a finger toward the sandy ground near the base. His eyes remained steadily on her.

Vivien moved closer, torn between looking at him and to where he pointed. There was nothing on the ground.

"I don't understand," Vivien whispered as she reached toward him. Heather's hand dropped from her shoulder.

Sam's energy tingled as she touched his form, not

MICHELLE M. PILLOW

unlike the flow of magic. She felt his love for her, love that had been etched in this very spot like an invisible signature only the stars could see.

"Yes, I'll marry you," her past words filtered through her thoughts, as if he wanted her to hear them the way he had the first time, with all the excitement and joy and certainty that they had felt at that moment.

He'd spun her until she'd fallen on the ground, and they'd ended up making love right there. They had been young and stupid, and it was only dumb luck that no one had seen them. Is that why he pointed at the ground? He wanted her to remember that moment with him?

Vivien nodded. "I remember, Sam. I remember all of it. I promise I won't forget."

Heather took Vivien's free hand and must have held onto Lorna with her other one because Vivien felt both of them through the connection.

"It's time, Viv," Heather said.

Vivien nodded. "I love you, Sam. I always will."

He smiled at her and again pointed toward the ground.

"I'll remember," she assured him.

His hand jerked a few times, repointing, as if biding her to look. Still, nothing was there.

As Heather and Lorna said the words to release his spirit, Vivien could only move her lips to mouth them. "Spirit you have been found pure. We release you into the light. Go in peace and love."

"Goodbye, Sam" She nearly choked on the words.

Sam's form blew into ash, scattering into the wind like the dying embers of a bonfire. Before he was completely gone, she heard him say, "Don't give up. You have so much of it to give."

This time his departure felt different, and she knew he had left her for good.

She took a deep breath. In many ways it felt like her first real breath in twenty years.

"He's gone," Vivien said. A feeling of peace settled over her where once sadness had lived. "For real this time."

"I felt him go too," Heather confirmed.

"Yeah, me too," Lorna agreed.

Vivien dropped to her knees and felt around the sand where Sam had pointed. She laid her hand on the surface, remembering the grainy texture against her naked body as they'd made love.

"What was he trying to tell you?" Heather asked.

"I think he wanted me to remember when he

proposed to me." Vivien smiled, taking a deep breath. "I can still feel him here."

Heather and Lorna joined her on the ground.

Heather scooped up a handful of sand and let it fall from between her fingers. "I don't know. There was something about the way he pointed."

"Hey, Lorna, do you feel anything here?" Heather patted the ground close to Vivien's hand. "Can you use your finding power to pick up any vibes about what Sam wanted Vivien to find?"

"I can try." Lorna leaned forward, lifting her hands toward the metal structure. To herself, she whispered, "What did Sam want Vivien to find?"

Vivien sat back to watch as Lorna lowered her palms and placed them on the ground.

Lorna swished her hands over the ground like a human metal detector before finally stopping. She swept some of the sand aside to mark a spot. "Here. Something is buried in the ground. We need to dig it out."

Vivien's breath caught in excitement. "He buried something for me?"

"There's only one way to find out," Heather said. She dug her hands into the ground and tossed the looser surface aside.

Vivien and Lorna joined her. They shoveled the

sand out of the hole with their hands. The ground became firmer and wetter the deeper they dug.

Vivien scooped her hands to lift as much as she could with one pass. Dirt packed under her fingernails, chipping them, but she kept going. Suddenly, a sharp pain sliced her finger as her skin slid over something buried about a foot into the ground.

"Ow!" She jerked her hand back. Blood dripped down her finger. "Oh, shit, that hurt."

"Let me see." Lorna tried to reach for her.

Vivien jerked her hand back, automatically knowing that Lorna was going to try to heal her and take the injury for herself. "No, you're not taking my pain. It's my cut. I'll deal with it."

"There's something buried." Heather reached into the hole and began digging around an object. "Once second. I think I can get it."

Heather leaned back on her knees, using her weight for leverage as she rocked back and forth to wiggle it loose. The ground released its hold, and Heather fell to the side. She caught herself with one hand and held a green glass bottle in another. Lifting the bottle toward Vivien, she said, "I think this is for you."

Vivien held the bottle to the sunlight. A piece of paper had been rolled within.

"A message in a bottle," Lorna stated.

"I used to look for them when we walked the shorelines. I told Sam that I would never be completely happy until I found one," Vivien said. "I was joking, of course, but..."

"He always wanted to make you happy," Heather said.

Vivien's hand shook. Some twisted metal wire held an old cork in place. It's what she'd cut herself on.

"Viv, you need to hold your finger up over your heart to slow the blood flow," Lorna said. "You're dripping."

Vivien obeyed, lifting her hand next to her shoulder as she made a fist to put pressure on the cut. She sat on the ground and put the bottle between her thighs as she untwisted the metal tie. The cork fell apart as she tried to pull it out.

Vivien handed the bottle to Heather. "Would you?"

Heather tried to dig the cork out before finally poking it down with her finger. It dropped into the bottle. She turned it upside-down and shook until the rolled paper bound with twine fell onto the ground. Heather pulled the string off before handing the message to Vivien.

"What does it say?" Lorna asked breathlessly.

Vivien unrolled two pieces of paper. On the top of the page in Sam's handwriting read, *"For Vivien."*

"They're song lyrics," Vivien said. He used to jot things down all the time in his notebook. She recalled some of them being quite terrible, but occasionally something beautiful came out of his rambling thoughts. Music notes were notated next to each line in Sam's shorthand to go with the words.

There is only us.
Only our hearts.
Or so it's been said.

Vivien's breath caught and she had to look away as she composed herself. She pressed the paper to her chest. She turned her attention back to the page.

But we did not plan on this.
How could we know?
The last moment would come.
I'll be watching you.

"Oh, Sam," Vivien whispered. She couldn't believe this bottle had been here waiting for her all this time. He'd loved the beach and must have hidden the bottle months before he died. The end had come so fast, and he'd never told her to look for it. If not for their new magical powers, she never would have found what Sam had left for her.

> *Save a piece of your heart for me.*
> *It's mine for always.*
> *But don't give up on love.*
> *You have so much of it to give.*
> *I want you to give it.*
> *I want you to feel.*
> *Think of me, and there will be only us.*
> *But you cannot come.*
> *Not yet.*
> *You must live.*

"All this time," Vivien whispered. "I'd misunderstood his last words. He had so much morphine in his system, and he wasn't making a lot of sense at the end. He must have been trying to tell me to look for this, but he only managed to mumble a few broken lyrics."

"May we see?" Heather asked.

Vivien handed her the first page. On the second was a short note.

She read aloud, "Dear Vivien, far be it from me

to argue with the women in your family, but now that I'm gone I guess I can have the last word. Our love is great and transcends time. I want nothing more than to stay with you forever, but how can I say I love you if I don't also wish for you to find what we have again should I not survive? The thought of you with another man is not one I will dwell on. Rather, I think of your smiling face and hope that he will treat you as you deserve. Find someone who can give you everything I no longer can. Settle for no less than everything. I love you, Viv. Forever, Sam."

Vivien rubbed her eyes with her sleeve to soak up the tears.

"I can't believe this was here all this time," Heather said, giving the lyrics back to Vivien.

"He probably thought he had more time to tell me where to look." Vivien gazed at the water. The sky had darkened, but late afternoon was just now turning to evening.

"I'll be watching you. Save your heart for me. It's mine."

In those last moments, his meaning had been lost. The memory she clung to had been unfinished. He wasn't telling her to wait for him. He was trying to give her his blessing to move on.

"I'll order a cab," Lorna said, nodding at Vivien's

bloody finger. She pulled out her phone and began pushing buttons to bring up the app. "We need to get that wound cleaned."

Vivien wasn't worried, but she knew Lorna couldn't turn off her mothering instincts. She lifted her arm as she held onto the papers. "Help me up?"

Lorna hooked Vivien under her arm and assisted her to her feet.

"I don't know about you ladies, but I'm emotionally drained," Vivien said. "And a little hungry."

Heather reached to brush the sand from Vivien's legs before standing and doing her own. "We should ask the driver to take us through a drive thru for dinner, but I'll do the ordering. Otherwise Vivien will think we need fifty hamburgers for three people."

Lorna picked up the glass bottle, wire, and piece of broken cork from the sand.

"We might need that many," Vivien protested. "It depends on how well they reheat later."

"Lorna, I'm really glad you're her roommate," Heather said. "Please make sure she starts eating things other than junk food."

"Oh, pie," Vivien inserted, ignoring Heather's playful lecture about her eating habits. "Yes, please make sure I eat plenty of your homemade pies."

"I'll bake you as many as you want," Lorna assured her with a laugh. She glanced at her phone app and pointed along the metal skeleton. "We need to go. The driver is on his way. He'll meet us up there."

CHAPTER FIFTEEN

Vivien watched Troy nod as William talked, enunciating his word with the metal spatula he wielded like a weapon over the barbeque grill. The men insisted on standing outside to guard over the burgers, even though it was chilly. She peeked at them through her bedroom window.

"Would you stop that?" Heather said from the doorway. "They're getting along fine. Stop worrying."

"Who said I was worried?" Vivien denied, not taking her eyes away.

"Only every sensation that Lorna and I pick up from you."

As your friend, I think it's my duty to tell you

when you're being creepy," Heather said. "Viv, you're being creepy. Drop the curtain and stop spying on Troy."

Vivien watched a few seconds longer before finally letting go of the curtain.

"Good girl. Come on, we should at least pretend to help Lorna in the kitchen," Heather said.

Vivien crossed her bedroom and joined Heather in the hallway. "You both really like him? You're not just saying that?"

"For a psychic you're not very intuitive about this." Heather stopped walking and put her hand on Vivien's arm. She let Vivien feel her emotions. "See. We really do like him. But what is most important is *you* really like him."

"I do." Vivien grinned. "Actually, I'm pretty sure I love him. I know it's only been a few weeks since I said goodbye to Sam, but..."

"Honey, that goodbye was twenty years in the making," Heather said. "I think I can speak for everyone when I say it's about damned time."

Vivien smiled as giddy excitement filled her.

"Have you told him how you feel yet?" Heather released her arm to stop the flow of emotional sharing.

"Not yet. I want to, but I don't know what it is about him that makes me so tongue-tied."

"You need to leap, Viv. If anything, we have all learned that life is too short to hold back."

"I'm nervous, you know." Vivien took a deep breath. It was difficult to explain. "With Troy, I can't read what he's feeling. I have no clue if he'll say I love you back. I honestly don't know how any of you do it."

"Do what?" Lorna asked, poking her head out of the kitchen.

"Function without psychic abilities," Heather said. "Vivien is feeling bad for those of us who can't usually read minds."

"I don't want to know what people are thinking," Lorna said. "If the dicky things people say online when they feel anonymous is any indication, I'm guessing it's best if they keep their innermost thoughts hidden deep, *deep* inside themselves."

Vivien chuckled. Her friend was not wrong.

"Are your psychic readings getting any easier to control?" Heather asked.

"My abilities are still growing—at least around everyone but Troy." Vivien moved toward the kitchen. Lorna stepped back to let her in the doorway. "I think I'm starting to get a handle on the flow

MICHELLE M. PILLOW

of information. And I have been seeing the future more, like clear pictures. It's a little scary."

"I don't think I want to see the future," Heather said.

Vivien grinned. "So, you're saying if there was a certain sexy contractor in your future, you wouldn't want to know about him?"

"Nice try," Heather dismissed. She went to the fridge and pulled out a pitcher of sweet tea. "I feel like the spirit world is calming down a little for me. The ghosts are still popping up, but they're talking less. Or maybe I'm getting better at spotting them and not showing I see them."

"It's actually kind of fun not being able to automatically tell what Troy's thinking all the time, or what kind of mood he's in unless he says the words."

"You need to tell him how you feel," Heather said.

"What did I miss?" Lorna studied them. "Did Viv finally admit that she loves—?"

Lorna instantly stopped talking when the door opened. She pretended to busy herself arranging hamburger buns on a plate.

"William hunt meat," William announced in a caveman's voice, grunting a few times as he carried his tray of burgers.

"You are such a dork," Vivien teased.

"Don't hate on me because you're jealous." William paused to kiss Lorna before setting the food down on the counter. "Food for my lady."

Heather set the pitcher next to the burgers and began pulling glasses out of the cupboard. She widened her eyes and nodded toward Troy. "Tell him."

"Am I missing something," he asked.

Vivien took his hand and led him to the living room. Bold patterns on her new couch matched the orange and red paintings she had hung. The room wasn't finished, but she was putting her own stamp on it.

"Is everything all right?" Troy's brow furrowed in concern.

"So here's the thing." Vivien took a deep breath.

"There's a thing?"

"Yes. There's a thing." She nodded.

"Okay."

"The thing is I tend to get locked in place. I can't explain why, but it happens. With my first husband, I was locked in the feeling that I could never really give myself to someone else because I loved him so much and was sure I'd never find it again."

Troy frowned and appeared to brace himself for where this conversation was going.

"Just listen." Vivien tried to hurry, but she wasn't used to explaining this part of herself. "With my second husband, I was locked in time. I didn't redecorate because I was afraid if I changed anything, I'd forget he was a tool and make the same mistakes again out of loneliness."

"Okay?" Troy appeared very confused. "So are you saying being with me is a mistake, and you can't love me?"

"No." She shook her head. "I'm saying I have a tendency to get locked, but I don't want to do that with you. I'm saying, maybe third time's a charm."

He blinked in surprise as if not expecting the conversation to turn the way it did. "I'm sorry, what? Did you say...?"

"I love you," she repeated. "And it's driving me a little crazy because I can't tell how you feel. So I need you to tell me."

"Are you asking me to marry you?" Troy asked, arching a brow. "I mean, it sounded like you were trying to. You said first husband, second husband, third time's a charm."

"No. I'm saying I love you." Vivien gave him a light smack on the chest. "Do you love me?"

He smiled. "You know, you keep telling me about these psychic visions you have, but I'm beginning to doubt they exist."

Vivien frowned.

"I swear I'm usually funny. You never get when I'm joking. Of course I believe in you. But how can you not know the answer to your question?" Troy cupped her cheek. "You have to know I'm crazy about you. It has to be pretty obvious."

"I know he's crazy about you, Viv," William yelled from the kitchen, proving he'd been eavesdropping. "Not sure why, but he is. No accounting for taste, I guess—"

"William," Heather scolded. The sound of a scuffle followed.

"Ow, what?" William demanded. "I'm helping."

Vivien shook her head. "Sorry about them."

"Don't be. I like them." Troy pulled her against him. "And I love you, Vivien Stone, and someday you're going to propose to me for real."

"Oh, am I?"

"Yep." He nodded, leaning down to kiss her. Against her lips, he said, "You don't have to be psychic to figure that one out."

The End

The Magical Fun Continues!

Lorna's Story:

Order of Magic Book 1: Second Chance Magic

Heather's Story:

Order of Magic Book 3: The Fourth Power

SECOND CHANCE MAGIC
ORDER OF MAGIC BOOK 1

*Secrets broke her heart... and have now come back
from the grave to haunt her.*

So far, Lorna Addams' forties are not what she
expected. After a very public embarrassment, she
finds it difficult to trust her judgment when it comes
to new friendships and dating. She might be willing
to give love a second chance when she meets the
attractive William Warrick, if only she could come to
terms with what her husband did to her and leave it
in the past.

How is a humiliated empty nest widow supposed
to move on with her life? It's not like she can develop
a sixth sense, séance her ex back, force him to tell her
why and give her closure. Or can she?

THE FOURTH POWER
ORDER OF MAGIC BOOK 3

Heather Harrison sees ghosts. It's not something she brags about. In fact, she wished she didn't. Communicating (or not communicating) with the dead only leads to heartache, and for her it led to a divorce. For the most part, she's happy being single. She's got a good business, close friends, and a slightly overprotective brother. What more does a forty-something woman need?

When her two best friends beg her for help in contacting loved ones, against her better judgment she can't say no to the séance. But some gateways shouldn't be opened, and some meddling spirits shouldn't be stirred...like that of her Grandma who insists she's "found her a nice man".

The supernaturals have come out to play and it's up to this amateur medium to protect herself and her friends before the danger they summoned comes to bite them in the backside.

NEWSLETTER

To stay informed about when a new book in the series installments is released, sign up for updates:

Sign up for Michelle's Newsletter

michellepillow.com/author-updates

ABOUT MICHELLE M. PILLOW

New York Times & USA TODAY
Bestselling Author

Michelle loves to travel and try new things, whether it's a paranormal investigation of an old Vaudeville Theatre or climbing Mayan temples in Belize. She believes life is an adventure fueled by copious amounts of coffee.

Newly relocated to the American South, Michelle is involved in various film and documentary projects with her talented director husband. She is mom to a fantastic artist. And she's managed by a dog and cat who make sure she's meeting her deadlines.

For the most part she can be found wearing pajama pants and working in her office. There may or may not be dancing. It's all part of the creative process.

∾

Come say hello! Michelle loves talking with readers on social media!

www.MichellePillow.com

facebook.com/AuthorMichellePillow

twitter.com/michellepillow

instagram.com/michellempillow

bookbub.com/authors/michelle-m-pillow

goodreads.com/Michelle_Pillow

amazon.com/author/michellepillow

youtube.com/michellepillow

pinterest.com/michellepillow

COMPLIMENTARY MATERIAL

THE SAVAGE KING
BY MICHELLE M. PILLOW

Lords of the Var® Book One
by Michelle M. Pillow

Bestselling Catshifter Romance Series

Cat-shifting King Kirill knows he must do his duty by his people. When his father unexpectedly dies, it's his destiny to take the throne and all of the responsibility that entails. What he hadn't prepared for is the troublesome prisoner that's now his to deal with.

Undercover Agent Ulyssa is no man's captive. Trapped in a primitive forest awaiting pickup, she's going to make the best out of a bad situation...which doesn't include falling for the seductions of a king.

~

The Savage King Excerpt

Kirill watched the door to his bedroom open. He'd been sitting in the dark, trying to relieve the stress headache that had built behind his eyes for the last week. The pain started at the base of his skull and radiated up to his temples until he could hardly see straight.

A heavy responsibility had been thrust on his shoulders, a responsibility he really hadn't prepared himself for, the welfare of the Var people. King Attor had not left him in a good position. He'd rallied the people to the brink of war, convinced them that the Draig were their enemy, and even went so far as to attack the Draig royal family.

Kirill wanted to see peace in the land. However, he knew the facts didn't bode well for it. The Draig had a long list of grievances against King Attor and the Var kingdom.

Before his death, the king had ordered an attack on the four Draig princes, all of which ended horribly for the Var. The worst was when Prince Yusef was stabbed in the back, a most cowardly embarrassment for the Var guard who did it. If he hadn't been executed in the Draig prisons, he would've been ostracized from the Var community. Luckily, Prince Yusef survived or they'd already be at battle.

Attor had also arranged for the kidnapping of Yusef's new bride. The Draig Princess Olena had been rescued, or that too would've led to war. The old king had even tried to poison Princess Morrigan, the future Draig queen, on two separate occasions. She too lived. And those were only a few of the offenses Kirill knew about in the few weeks before King Attor's death. He could just imagine what he didn't know.

Kirill sighed, feeling very tired. He'd known since birth that the day would come when he'd be expected to step up and lead the Var as their new king. He just hadn't expected it to be for another hundred or so years. His father had been a hard man, whom he'd foolishly believed was invincible.

"Here kitty, kitty, kitty." His lovely houseguest's whisper drew his complete attention from his heavy thoughts.

Ulyssa bent over like she expected him to answer to the insulting call. He dropped his fingers from his temple into his lap, and a quizzical smile came to his lips. As he watched her, he wasn't sure if he was angered or amused by her words.

"Are you in here, you little furball?" she said, a little louder.

She wore his clothes. Never had the outfit looked sexier. His jaw tightened in masculine interest, as he unabashedly looked her over. All too well did he remember the softness of her body against his and the gentle, offering pleasure of her sweet lips. She'd made soft whimpering noises when he'd touched her, yielding, purring sounds in the back of her throat. Even with the aid of nef, he was surprised by how easily and confidently she melted into him. The Var were wild, passionate people and were drawn to the same qualities in others. He suspected she'd be an untamed lover.

Too bad she'd belonged to his father first. In his mind, that made her completely untouchable though none would dare question his claim if he were to take her to his bed. Technically, by Var law, she belonged to him until he chose to release her. For an insane moment, he thought about keeping her as a lover. He knew he wouldn't, but the thought was entertaining.

Kirill's grin deepened. Ulyssa strode across his home to the bathroom door with an irritated scowl. It was obvious she didn't see him in the darkened corner, watching her. He detected her engaging smell from across the room, the smell of a woman's desire. It stirred his blood, making his limbs heavy with arousal. And, for the first time since his father's death, his headache relieved itself.

"Hum, maybe I'm looking too high. I'm sure there has to be a little cat door here somewhere. Come here, little kitty. Where are you hiding?"

His slight smile fell at her words. It was easy to detect her mocking tone.

"Where's your little kitty door, huh?" Ulyssa whispered to herself, her blue gaze searching around in the dark.

Kirill grimaced in further displeasure. He watched her open the door to his weapons cabinet. Her eyes rounded, and he thought she might take one. She didn't. Instead, she nodded in appreciation before closing the door and continuing her search for an exit.

She stopped at a narrow window by his kitchen doorway. Her neck craned to the side, as she tried to see out over the distance. Kirill knew she looked at the forest. From under her breath, he heard her vehement whisper, "Where exactly did you little fur balls bring me? Ugh, I need to get out of this flea trap, even if I have to fight every one of you cowardly felines to do it. I've fought species twice as big and three times as frightening. A couple of little kitty cats don't scare me."

If this insolent woman wanted to play tough, oh, he'd play. Curling gracefully forward, Kirill shifted before his hands even touched the ground. He let one thick paw land silently on the floor, followed by a second. Short black fur rippled over his tanned flesh, blending him into the shadows. His clothes fell from his body, and he lowered his head as he crept forward. A low sound of warning started in the back of his throat. He was livid.

To find out more about Michelle's books
visit www.MichellePillow.com

PLEASE LEAVE A REVIEW
THANK YOU FOR READING!

Please take a moment to share your thoughts by reviewing this book.

Be sure to check out Michelle's other titles at www.MichellePillow.com

CPSIA information can be obtained
at www.ICGtesting.com
Printed in the USA
LVHW111039210821
695815LV00020B/458